MURDER DURING THE BITTER NIGHT

BLYTHE BAKER

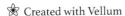

～

When Lillian Crawford is approached by a potential client with an unusual and dangerous request, Lillian and her brother are drawn into another game of shadows and deceit.

With Lillian pining for the elusive Eugene Osbourn and Felix struggling with secrets from the past, will the Crawford twins be too distracted to stop a murder before it occurs?

～

1

Thunder clapped.

I sat up straight, cold sweat clinging to my forehead.

Lightning flashed, casting long shadows across the floor. For a few seconds, brilliant white light as bright as day glowed through the windowpanes. The glass trembled as another roll of thunder came through, the sound filling the room as if a collision of giants was happening right outside.

My heart slammed against my chest, my breath came in shallow pants as the room was plunged back into the pitch black of darkness.

I blinked against the shadows, as thick as velvet in front of my eyes.

Where am I?

What day was it? What was the last thing I remembered?

Felix. Eugene Osbourn. Cousin Richard.

...A lifeless corpse.

I clapped my hands over my eyes, and rubbed them furiously, as if I could scrub away that last, unpleasant memory.

What had woken me? Thunder? No...it had been something else.

A scream?

I tried to swallow, but my throat was as dry as parchment. Light splashed into the room again, like the flicker of a candle that was quickly snuffed out. My desk stood along the back wall. My wardrobe stood with one of the doors slightly open. A dress lay across an ornate chair near the door.

I was in my room at Cousin Richard's estate.

Thunder rumbled outside again a moment later; the storm had begun to move away.

I shifted underneath the quilts and sheets, stretching my legs out as I willed my heart to slow, my mind beginning to clear.

We were at my cousin's country house near London. My dreams, however, had been filled with the long, broad corridors of my childhood home, back in New York.

Why had I briefly thought myself there again? It had been over two months now since Felix and I had taken ship all the way to England. I had not dreamt of home the entire time we had been here. I had barely even thought about New York, loving my time in England. Why had I dreamt of it now?

Wait...why did I awake? Something disturbed me. What was it?

Had it really been a scream?

I sat for a moment, listening hard, which was difficult given the wind whipping against the glass, the rain spattering the roof overhead. More lightning, more thunder... but no other sound outside of the usual bumps in the night.

It must have been in my dreams...

That was not terribly surprising, as I considered it. Life had been less than glamorous as of late, what with all the dangerous situations I seemed to keep finding myself involved in.

I lay back down in the bed. With the storm moving away, it would be easy enough to fall back asleep...if my thoughts would only settle down again.

Worry had fueled my mind into sharp focus, trying to understand the danger it had perceived me to be in. The thumping in my chest from my heart might have eased, but the tension it had created remained behind. I could have run full laps around the house right then and not even broken a sweat.

Well...not any more of a sweat than I already had endured.

Calm yourself, Lillian. Everything is fine.

I was safe, I was all right.

I told myself to relax, forcing my muscles to release the tension. I wouldn't sleep otherwise, I knew.

Everything had been quiet over the past few days, a relief after all that the members of our household had recently been through. During a short stay on the estate of some acquaintances, who were relatives of my friend Eugene Osbourn, a violent crime had occurred. Although the culprit had ultimately been apprehended by my twin brother Felix and me, it had been a distressing business for everyone.

Afterward, we had decided to end our stay early,

despite our hosts' insistence that we could remain. We felt as if we had overstayed our welcome, and we knew that the whole trip was tainted by the ordeal. It was all anyone could think about. Eugene had reluctantly agreed with me, and I knew that even though his aunt and uncle had apologized for doubting me, they all needed time to heal after what had happened.

And so, my cousin Richard, his children, my brother, and I had returned to Richard's estate, and while Felix and I were quite relieved, our young second cousins were anything but. Gloria and Marie had done everything they could not to remain in the same room as me, and had taken to calling me the angel of death so that I might hear it. Marie may have just been going along with her older sister, trying to remain on her good side, but I doubted she wholly disagreed with her; the frightened look in her eyes told me as much.

Richard, likewise, had taken a cool attitude toward Felix and me, despite the fact we had solved the recent case. It seemed as if his thoughts were not too far from his daughters', and he wanted nothing more than for life to return to normal.

I wanted the very same, I had assured him, but it was as if he did not believe me.

He even went so far as to mutter something under his breath about understanding "*our parents' frustrations,*" or some such nonsense.

Regardless, we had been back in Richard's home for some days, and life appeared entirely uneventful now. Felix had picked up his classes again, and I agreed to continue my art lessons with Gloria and Marie.

The only person who acted halfway interested in

treating my brother and me the same as always was William, who seemed to think Felix was some sort of hero. There was hardly a moment in the day when William did not ask to tag along with my brother if he could, often simply appearing as if from thin air.

Felix liked the boy's attention. I suspected it was because William reminded him of our younger brother Daniel in a way.

At least, the way that Daniel might have been, had he not harbored such inner darkness...and had he not died many years ago.

I closed my eyes, some of the worry beginning to ebb away. Richard would soon set aside recent unfortunate events, as would Marie and Gloria. Soon, our usual banter would return, as would the parties and the social obligations. Life would begin again, and Felix and I could move on.

It did sadden me, in a way, not to be as close to Eugene as I had grown accustomed to during our visit to his relations. I found I rather missed knowing that I would run into him at breakfast, or perhaps have a stroll with him through the gardens along the swimming pond. I would no longer need to care so much about how perfectly my black, bobbed hair had been combed, or if the dress I had chosen for the day flattered my figure well enough.

Well, if the rumors I heard during our visit were true... perhaps a certain conversation will be happening soon enough.

But how could I be certain whether he meant to propose marriage? And why had he decided to take as long to do so as he had? If he had made up his mind, why would he delay in speaking with me about any future plans we might wish to make together?

I wrinkled my nose, and rolled over onto my side as light briefly shimmered against the opposite wall from the lightning, like the reflection of sunlight glinting off the surface of a lake. At first, I had been annoyed to hear gossip of such a union between Eugene Osbourn and me. Now, I was annoyed that he had yet to approach me about it.

I allowed myself one guilty moment to consider him, his handsome face, his lithe form. He had long, narrow fingers, the perfect sort for playing piano as he did so well. A small smile spread across my face as I thought of the few nights before the tragedy, wherein Eugene would play and entertain us all, while his cousins sang along. Music did run in that family, and it seemed to be a dominant trait.

Perhaps I could telephone or even send a note to him...just to inquire after him and thank his relatives again for allowing our visit.

I frowned, counting the days we had been apart on the tips of my fingers.

Was it too soon? Would that not seem desperate?

Maybe not desperate...maybe he would see it as confirmation that I am as interested in him as he is in me.

What might his uncle say, though? I knew that his family would have a lot of sway in whether or not Eugene would pursue an engagement with me. I might have redeemed my reputation with Mr. Pearl in regards to investigating murders, but would that also ensure that he would encourage his nephew in any proposal?

I chewed the end of my fingernail. It seemed as if

Eugene and I walked on a knife's edge, and one good push could cause our entire relationship to go one way or the other. His uncle had told him to reconsider, and I had seen some of the worry in Eugene's eyes afterward. Had he truly thought it over once more?

I thought back to his attitude toward me the last day or two we had been at the Pearls' manor, whether or not he had changed toward me.

No...I would not say that he did.

In fact, before Felix had interrupted one conversation of ours, Eugene had been close to telling me something, hadn't he? He had begun by saying that he knew we had met for a reason. I agreed. But there had been something else...something more he wanted to say that he never got the chance to before my departure.

What was he going to tell me?

Maybe I *would* send him a letter, first thing in the morning. Surely I could find some excuse to write.

If there truly was something there between the pair of us, and it was not entirely an invention of my mind, then no one would think anything of it, would they? Everyone else seemed to be talking about it around us, everyone else seemed to see it...but we just kept having to put the conversation on hold, didn't we?

Perhaps it was time to address it.

Determination filled my mind, but I urged it to settle down as I closed my eyes once again. *There, now, there will be plenty of time for all that come morning. I can spend half the day writing the perfect letter, if I so choose –*

Another scream pierced the night.

This time I was certain it was not a nightmare. I sat straight up again, my heart pounding.

I leapt out of bed, my skin tingling, the tips of my fingers going numb.

The cry had come from a man. That much was certain.

I hurried to the door, yanked it open, and flew out into the darkness. Only then did I realize the scream had come from the other side of the hall.

Felix!

I dashed across the hall, the tip of my toe catching on the edge of the rug that ran the length of the corridor. I threw my hands out in front of me to catch myself –

My palms collided with the door, and pain shot up the length of my arms. I winced, but stood upright and fumbled for the door handle.

It gave easily, thankfully unlocked.

I rushed inside, just as a lightning strike outside the window sent blinding light flashing across the room... revealing Felix's still form splayed out across his bed.

He wasn't moving.

Thunder echoed through the whole manor, making the very walls tremble. It seemed another cell of the storm had come through, and with double the strength of the first one.

I took a nervous step into the room, my heart somewhere behind me on the floor of the corridor. I watched his chest. I could not see any movement.

Not another death...no...

Standing in the doorway would do me no good, would do him no good, so I made my way to him.

A horrendous snore nearly made me jump out of my skin. I grabbed one of the bed posts for support, my heart trying to beat out of my ribcage.

Felix let out a long breath, and rolled over onto his side.

I slumped down onto the bed beside him to catch my breath.

Felix grunted, and drew his arms in but didn't wake.

Restless, again...

It was a wonder the storm didn't disturb him, but growing up in New York, we had our fair share of thunderstorms in the summertime. In truth, it wasn't the storm that had woken me, but his screams.

I sighed, shaking my head. The nightmares seemed to be plaguing him more frequently as of late, and it did not seem that we could do anything to stop them. We had tried everything; drinking warm milk before bed, staying awake reading until he could no longer keep his eyes open, trying to do some light exercise just before dinner. Nothing helped.

Not that I had ever really expected it to, because what we were working against was much stronger than what most people would have to fight against when it came to battling nightmares. We had recently dealt with another murder, after all.

I glanced at Felix, who seemed to be sleeping soundly now. I could not entirely relax, however, worrying that he might let out yet another yell; they came so sporadically.

My heart had begun to slow again, but now I wondered if I would ever be able to get back to sleep. Two frights in one night...and I didn't even know what time it actually was.

I lifted the heels of my palms to my eyes, rubbing them vigorously. Given how my eyes ached and the stiffness in my shoulders, I could only assume it was three or four in the morning. Still too early to rise, yet plenty of time to lie awake in the dark.

Maybe I should just sit with him for a while...make sure he's all right.

It was something I'd done frequently enough as a child. When Felix had nightmares after Daniel's death, I would sit up with him until he fell asleep. I often couldn't sleep, even now, until I knew that he had done so. Only then could I relax fully.

I wondered if he would ever grow out of these.

Not likely until the dangers around us stop.

...But would they?

I could see how much it tormented him. He might be willing to stand with me, and help me solve crimes...but it was clear that they stuck with him more than they did with me.

For me, detective work had brought a great deal of opportunity. Not only to further myself and my reputation, but also it had brought people into my life that I likely never would have met before. More than that, it had brought a new sense of confidence and purpose, a realization that I did not have to live as some silly creature flitting from one party to the next in the season's most fashionable attire. I had intelligence and skill, and I could use them to find answers for people whose lives had been torn apart by violence, and to make the world a slightly safer place for others. I could do something that mattered.

There was no denying the fact that I had a knack for

investigating crimes. I understood people, as did Felix. We made a great team. Even Eugene Osbourn and I worked well together.

And I had survived thus far, hadn't I? Even finding myself in the most dangerous of situations, I had made it out alive. It might have been close a time or two, but here I sat, still living.

Felix drew in a deep breath, and I looked over, wondering if he was rousing. He simply adjusted, rolling over onto his stomach. I took hold of the corner of the quilt, and pulled it back up over his shoulder.

If unearthing people's darkest secrets and capturing killers had turned out to be a good line of work for me, I was less sure it was good for Felix. Such situations forced him to face the shadows of his past, to wrestle with his memories of the long ago night our younger brother Daniel had died.

Felix might have come to a place where he had been able to forgive himself for what happened all those years ago, but the most recent murder we had investigated had seemed all too familiar to him, rooted in the darkness brooding inside the members of Eugene's family. Our deceased brother, too, had possessed a dark side.

It was something I never would have imagined for our family. I had always known that Daniel could be devious, even nasty when he did not get his way, but to have gone so far as to try and lure Felix to his death? What must that have done to Felix, all these years, recalling how he had been forced to kill or be killed in self defense? I could hardly imagine.

Well, that's not really true anymore, is it? I have faced down my share of deadly situations of late.

Perhaps my twin and I were more alike now. Maybe he was not such a stranger as I had begun to fear.

Felix had settled down enough, it seemed.

Thunder growled in the distance; it sounded as if we really had come to the end of the storm. Rain tip-tapped on the window, slow and steady, the perfect sound for sleep.

I wandered back to my own room, taking care to go quietly so as not to wake Felix on my way out. I considered telling him about the nightmares, but knew that come morning, I would choose to leave him in blissful ignorance. He did not need to be reminded of it if he could not remember it himself.

I closed my bedroom door behind me, and let out another long sigh. My heart weighed heavily within me, and though exhaustion still lingered after the travel and the investigation at Eugene's family's estate, I knew that sleep would likely not come for the rest of the night for me. My mind had already spent far too much time awake, considering too many difficult truths.

I slid into bed all the same, hoping I might find some semblance of rest. My room was still cool and dark, comfortable enough for a few hours more of sleep. My bed, soft. My blankets, warm and cozy.

I should have been able to relax but, for some reason, a nameless uneasiness nagged at the back of my mind, like the thunder that wouldn't stop rumbling in the distance. I was tired of these damp, cold days...but something told me we were far from done with them.

More darkness lay ahead.

2

"I thought you should know that I intend to put my name in the newspaper," I said, in a rather matter of fact tone the following morning at breakfast. "Along with an advertisement for my private investigative services."

Rain slammed against the estate, battering the windows like tiny rocks, nearly drowning out the sound of the crackling fireplace. The sky outside appeared as dark as the hour of twilight, the clouds lying as heavy and thick as a wool blanket over the earth.

Cousin Richard folded the top half of his newspaper with the tips of his fingers, his eyes fixing on me over the paper and ink. He arched a brow, his expression less than thrilled. "Is that so?"

I nodded. "I have spent a great deal of time considering this, and I think it's the right decision."

Gloria, the second cousin who was nearest to me in age, gave a disgusted click of her tongue. I turned to see her sitting across the table, crossing her arms, looking over at her younger sister with a roll of her eyes.

"I think it's a good idea," said William from his father's right side. He gave me a definitive nod. "She can help people, like she helped me, and helped Mr. Osbourn."

"Precisely my thought, William," I said, nodding in return.

Richard regarded his son with mild curiosity before looking back to me. "You are certain about this?"

"I am," I said.

"She's put a great deal of thought into it," Felix said from the seat beside me. We had discussed my decision at length that morning after he had awoken. He supported me in the continuation of my investigative work, even though I could see some reservation in his eyes. He reminded me of the independence this could grant me from Mother and Father, something I had not readily considered. He was right, of course. The ability to generate my own income, relying on my own skill, instead of being reliant on an allowance from our parents, would be very freeing.

"Have you considered all the repercussions?" Richard asked, folding his paper and setting it aside. "The cost alone, perhaps? Where do you intend to get the money for expenses?"

"I saved a little of the fee Mrs. Burke paid me some weeks ago for finding her brother's killer," I said. "This is not something I would ask you to take care of for me, I assure you."

Richard rubbed his hand over his chin, looking down at his empty plate. What must have been a relatively leisurely morning for him had just taken a rather stressful turn.

"What makes you think anyone would answer your advertisement?" Gloria hissed.

I looked coolly across the table at her. "Might I remind you that Mrs. Burke sought me out after hearing about my previous successes? I did not even need to put up an advertisement, and she came to me, based on my reputation. Imagine the sort of clientele I could attract if more people only knew that I was here, available for them to consult?"

"And you *want* to do this?" Marie asked, sounding aghast. "You want to look at murder scenes and dead bodies all day long? What is wrong with you?"

"Nothing is wrong with me," I said. "I am making myself useful...and happen to be profiting by it. Think of how many crimes must take place in a city as large as London. I could have endless opportunities, endless money flowing in. Felix and I could form a very successful business, all on our own."

All without our parents' help, and that alone could be worth it, just as Felix said.

Richard let out a heavy exhale, shaking his head. "I still wonder if you have considered all that this will entail," he said. "You might attract the wrong sort of clients, those who will consider you more of a mercenary out for hire."

"I will not be doing any dirty work, if that's what you're implying," I said. "I will have the discretion of accepting clients or not. It will be entirely my choice."

"But as you yourself have sometimes said, Lillian, we do not always know even those closest to us," Richard said, his eyes narrowing. "How can you be certain that you would be taking on savory clients?"

I folded my arms. "Then I shall come to you, and see if you are aware of them."

Richard shook his head. "No, I will not take part in this. If you need outside help, then I do not think this is the right direction for you."

"It is not as if I can do it *entirely* alone," I said. "You have helped me in the past."

"I have, and I have sworn off it," Richard said. "I cannot keep stepping into these sorts of situations. I do not think my health can handle it, nor can my children."

I surveyed the table, each of my cousins in turn...and guilt washed over me.

It was true that I had dragged Richard and his family into my troubles more than once, sometimes at a risk to Richard's reputation.

"I'm sorry," I said, swallowing my frustration as swiftly as I could. "I do not wish to frustrate or upset you any further. If you truly wish for me to refrain, then I will."

"Do not listen to her, Father, she is lying," Gloria said crossly. "She will go ahead and do it anyway and just not tell you."

"When have I ever given you the impression that *I* am a liar?" I asked, my anger quickly returning.

Gloria opened her mouth to retort when Richard held up his hand to stop her. His brow furrowed, but it was clear he was trying to gather himself. "I have never called you a liar, Lillian, and it would be wise for everyone else to follow suit," he said, shooting a look over at his daughter. "I appreciate the thoughtfulness, and I am inclined to believe that you are telling the truth, though I also wonder if there is not some ulterior motive behind your sudden relent."

My eyes narrowed. "You may not call me a liar, but you think me to be akin to some conniving child? Trying to pull the wool over your eyes?" I asked. I clicked my tongue in frustration. "Hardly. I am simply attempting to acknowledge the fact that you have been incredibly generous to Felix and me. My desire is that we would not do anything to sabotage you again."

"You have never sabotaged me," Richard said with a note of defeat.

"You think my words to be less than genuine – " I started.

"We are sorry, Richard," Felix said. "We truly are grateful for the way you have opened your home to us. We realize these unfortunate circumstances have put you into uncomfortable situations. We do not wish to do that to you, as it feels a rather poor payment for your generosity."

"Exactly," I said, exasperated that my twin had managed to phrase my thoughts better than I.

Richard looked away. "Setting my worries aside, I must recognize that you have indeed helped several local families, not just our own. It is an honorable undertaking, and I must commend you both for that," he said.

He paused, considering his words. "And so, I cannot say that you are wrong in your plans. Nor can I prevent you from doing as you wish, as you are both adults and I am not your father, nor even an uncle. But if you do choose to pursue this path, and I would advise that you seriously consider it further...please leave my family and me out of it all. In the past, you have consulted me about suspects or other such things, but I would prefer that you allow me to remain ignorant of your exploits, in future. You will have my permission to take the chauffeur and the car wherever you need to go, and I will not ask questions. All I request is that it remains *your* business, and that you keep all of your investigating out of my home."

"I think that is entirely reasonable," I said. "And I would be more than happy to give you your space. I apologize that any of our prior investigations ever crossed that line."

Richard nodded. "Thank you for understanding. I do not think any of us can handle any more stress of the like."

"I can understand that," I said. "And respect it."

"As do I," said Felix.

"So we are in agreement, then?" I asked. "Felix and I shall continue to take on cases?"

"Yes," Richard said, though he seemed less comfortable when saying it so plainly.

"Good," I said. "And I will honor your request, and weigh the consequences."

FELIX and I did just as promised, and spent the afternoon considering all the worst possible outcomes. Even after we realized that our plans could possibly end with either of, or both, our deaths, we recognized that we could die in everyday life just as easily, and accepted what might come.

It excited me, thinking about making our endeavors a

bit more formal, considering all the possible clients that we could come across. Felix seemed more reserved, but he and I both knew that it was because of his discomfort with death in general.

"You have come a long way, you know," I told him as we looked over the paper we had been using to write up the reasons why we should not put the advertisement in the paper, a list which we had gone through already and found to be lacking sufficient weight to convince me otherwise. "When we encountered our first murder investigation, it nearly paralyzed you."

"Yes, I have been thinking that, too..." he said. "It is not as if the idea of seeing corpses is entirely normal or inconsequential to me, but at least I can stomach discussing matters with potential clients."

"I know how queasy crime scenes make you," I said. "For some reason, I can handle it better."

"Then I will allow you to do so," Felix said. "If you give me the chance to take care of other things instead."

We drew up the advertisement, cleaned it up, and by the following morning had something to take down to the newspaper printer. We were promised the editor would receive it and look at it at his earliest convenience.

MY IMPATIENCE GREW as I continued to look for our advertisement, only to find the morning paper lacking for two and a half weeks, all the way to the end of July. Every morning, I would sit as quietly as I could while Richard finished the paper. As the days went on, he began to notice that I asked for the paper as soon as he was finished, and that I would quickly scroll through and then cast it away with frustration.

Thankfully, the advertisement appeared on the second to last day of the month, and I let out an exclamation as I found it, jumping to my feet. "Finally!" I said, my voice carrying across the otherwise quiet breakfast table.

Gloria and Marie looked up from their plates, Gloria with a scathing look, Marie with one of innocent curiosity.

"Finally, it's here," I said, spreading the paper out over the table, pushing aside my plate and cutlery.

Felix stood beside me and peered down at the page. "My word, it's bigger than I would have expected."

"Perhaps we overpaid for it," I said dismissively. "No matter. It certainly gets the point across, doesn't it?"

Richard wiped his face and laid his napkin down before joining us. "That looks better than advertisements I've seen from some of the larger companies in this city," he said with a small smile. "Well done, you two."

"Thank you," I said.

"It looks a bit pretentious, doesn't it?" Gloria asked, leaning over the table to inspect the paper.

"I think it's anything but," I said, glaring at her.

"Of course you would," she said. "You wrote it."

"It doesn't describe exactly what you do," Marie said.

"That doesn't matter," Felix said. "They will understand what services we offer with the title of private investigators. Only those who have real trouble will reach out to us."

"What if someone calls you to find their lost puppy?" Gloria asked.

"Or what if someone sends you on a wild goose chase for nothing?" Marie asked.

I rolled my eyes. "I am sure we will receive those sorts of requests. However, we are only going to take those cases that seem real and urgent."

"And how will you know?" Gloria asked.

I furrowed my brow. "If someone comes to us about a violent crime, we will take the time to listen, of course."

The next morning, I waited to see if the butler, Hughes, would bring the mail. When he did, I pretended to be invested in my broiled tomatoes and toast while he delivered letters to Richard. He then left the room without a word to us.

"I assume that nothing arrived for Felix and me?" I asked as casually as I could.

"Not today," Richard said. "My apologies."

I didn't much care for the gratified sneer that Gloria wore across the table from me, as I tried not to consider the possibility that all my plans would come to nothing.

What, I wondered, were people waiting for? Surely someone, somewhere must be in need of help?

As the first week of August passed by, I grew more and more frustrated, feeling as if life had become nothing more than anxious waiting.

"It will do you no good to pace around here, day in and day out," Felix said to me one stormy afternoon. "It's best to just let it be what it will be."

"Am I supposed to simply forget it?" I snapped, rounding on him as he sat across from William at the chess set once again. They had taken to spending their afternoons from lunch until tea time playing, as the rains had made it nearly impossible for them to go out and enjoy the lake for swimming.

"Yes," Felix said with an exasperated chuckle. "You cannot will any letters or calls to come for us."

I frowned and sat down, picking up a book and trying to focus on it.

"And you can stop that angry sighing whenever you would like," Felix added.

I groaned, looking up and shooting him a nasty look.

William snickered.

"What if this was nothing more than a waste of time and money?" I asked, snapping the book shut as quickly as I had opened it and tossing it onto the sofa beside me.

"Then we will know that we tried and nothing came of it," Felix said. "There was no guarantee going into this that we would even garner anyone's attention."

I exhaled sharply. "No, but I would have *assumed* that – "

"That's the problem right there, isn't it?" Felix asked. "When does assuming anything ever end well for anyone?"

"Well...never, I suppose," I said, turning my nose up. "Nevertheless, I am surprised that when we made no public statement about our endeavors, we attracted clients. Now that we advertise our services, it's utterly silent."

"Then perhaps we can take it as a good thing?" Felix asked, moving his bishop into place for his next turn where he would capture one of William's knights. "It could mean there are simply no crimes happening around London. Maybe we have ensured a time of peace for the city as a whole. We should be rejoicing."

I raised an eyebrow, glaring at him.

He grinned at me, and William chuckled again.

"How could someone as young as you find the subject of murder humorous?" I asked William. "Your father will surely have my tongue for even speaking of these things in your presence..."

"Perhaps you have forgotten, cousin, but you promised you would hire me as your assistant one day," William said with a slight twinkle in his eyes. "Of course I don't think you truly meant it."

"Well, I don't know about that," Felix said with a grin. "You're quite a sharp young fellow. Why do you think I've been playing chess with you so much? If we end up attracting as many clients as Lillian hopes we will, then we are going to need a third member of our party as soon as possible. When can you start?"

William laughed.

"I suppose you are right about there being no cause for impatience..." I said. "If we wanted to, we could always post the advertisement again."

"Right," Felix said. "That's the positive way to look at it."

"I had really hoped we would have heard something by now, though," I said.

"I know," Felix said. "You are hoping you made the right choice, and someone coming to you with a new case would vindicate our decision."

"While I do not much care for your particular choice of words, I do agree with the sentiment," I said with a great sigh. "Besides...I was hoping I could inform Mother of our newest business venture the next time I wrote her. If we have no cases and no clients, I cannot very well say that we are a success."

"Father won't much like it anyway," Felix said. "He will demand we stop it at once."

"I know," I said. "But what can he do, as far away as he is? Besides, he should be pleased, what with you taking classes that Richard has arranged, and me sitting in on some painting lessons with Gloria and Marie."

"Don't forget Mr. Osbourn," William said.

I blinked at him. "What of him?"

"Your engagement," William said. "Oh, my apologies. Your *coming* engagement. Marie told me about it."

My eyes narrowed. "You pay more attention than I might have given you credit for. What else has Marie said?"

William considered, looking up and tapping his chin. "Not much else. Nothing I didn't already know." Then his eyes widened. "But did you know about Marie and Oswald?"

I smirked. "Eugene Osbourn's cousin?"

William nodded. "When we were staying with the Pearls, I caught the two of them talking out in the garden, standing very close together." He leaned forward, and dropped his voice to a whisper. "I think he kissed her."

I let out a convincing gasp. "...No!"

William nodded. "Father doesn't know, because Marie told me she would throw my favorite tin soldier out into the lake if I said anything."

"Don't worry too much, William. I think your father will learn soon enough if Oswald proposes to her," Felix said.

"You think he will propose to her?" William asked. He shook his head, then. "Poor Gloria. She will be terribly jealous."

I laughed. "William, you are keenly perceptive of people and their feelings. I am pleased to see that this trait runs in our family."

William beamed at the compliment.

The door to the drawing room opened, and Marie's face appeared around the door. "The mail has arrived, and a letter has come for you." She held it out around the door.

My heart leapt within me, and I hurried toward her. "Finally!" I took it from her. "Who is it from?"

"I don't know," Marie said. "Hughes simply said it was odd that it had arrived in the middle of the afternoon.

I turned it over in my hands, noting the lack of any return address, and felt two things at once. At first, disappointment. A small part of me had been hoping it would be from Eugene. I hadn't followed my earlier resolution to write to him, so I could hardly blame him for failing to reach out either. Still, I had hoped... I would have recognized his writing at once, however, and the rather sprawling script across the front of the envelope did not belong to him. That was when I realized it had to be from someone we did not know, and therefore, likely someone answering our advertisement. Disappointment turned to excitement.

I nearly hopped back over to the sofa, where I sat and began to peel open the letter. Felix joined me, peering over my shoulder.

"Well?" he asked.

"One moment, one moment," I said.

I had barely opened the letter before Felix spoke again. "It's from an anonymous writer," he said.

I glared at him. "How did you already – " I quickly looked down toward the bottom of the note, and found his words to be true. There was no signature.

"Read it!" William said, sitting up on his knees expectantly as if waiting for a bedtime story.

I licked my lips, and looked back down at the letter.

Dear Mr. and Miss Crawford,

Your advertisement could not have come at a better time. I would like to set up a discreet meeting with you, but will not be disclosing my name just yet, so as to protect my privacy. I also will not be filling you in on the details of the situation, as I fear that if this letter is intercepted, my identity will become clear. My family is being watched, and I cannot be too careful.

I looked up at Felix, my heart quickening. "The family is being watched, hmm? This certainly sounds promising."

"Promising?" Marie asked, sounding horrified. "How could you say that?"

"If you were here a few minutes ago, you would have known that she was hoping for a case," William answered for Felix and me.

"Go on, keep reading," Felix said.

I continued.

All I can tell you is that time is of the essence, as I fear the danger my family is in. If you would be willing, please send a response to the following address, with a time and place to meet in one of the London parks.

I glanced at the address below, my brow furrowing. "Our response should be sent to a public library? Where presumably this person has arranged for it to be passed on to them?"

"That's odd," Felix said, scratching his chin. "Though I suppose if they are hoping to keep their identity private, this might be the best way."

"True," I said. "Well? What should we say?"

"Finish the letter," Felix said, nodding toward the page in my hand.

I looked back down at it. *You will know me by my cobalt blue hat. I will find a seat alone, and I often am fond of bringing scraps of bread to feed the ducks.*

"Not terribly helpful, is it?" William asked. "How often do I see people feeding the ducks at the park?"

"I think that's precisely the point," I said. "That way no one will suspect them."

"Whatever it is that is troubling them must truly be serious, otherwise I do not think they would be going to such lengths to maintain their anonymity," Felix said.

"Yes, I think you might very well be right," I said. "There are two final lines here."

If you have not already been inundated with other troubles from other people, I beg that you would answer my letter as soon as you possibly can. I will be waiting, and thank you in advance for your help.

Felix exhaled through his nose, looking over at me. "What do you think?"

"I think we should take it," I said.

"We don't know anything apart from the fact that a family is in danger," Felix said. "And they are being watched, I suppose."

"Shouldn't that be enough for us to want to help them?" I asked.

"Do you really want to help them? Or just to make a bigger name for yourself?"

The question came from Marie, which surprised me. I met her gaze, and saw a glint of anger in her eyes.

"I thought you understood me better than that," I said. "I assume Gloria has been feeding you some nonsense about me only wishing to better my reputation?"

Marie didn't answer immediately, but with a swish of her dress, spun away from me like a pouting child who had been found out.

"I don't know what you are talking about," she said.

I rolled my eyes. "Don't give me that ridiculousness. Your sister has little faith in me, I know, but you? I thought that you and I had begun to understand one another, Marie."

Marie's face flushed scarlet, but she said nothing.

I sighed. "I realize your loyalty naturally remains with your sister, but I would hope that you would give me the chance to prove myself. Did you not hear anything I said to your father?"

"Gloria says you were lying," Marie said.

"Yes, I was there," I said. "Unless she's repeated that since."

Marie said nothing.

"I wouldn't worry too much about it," Felix said with a shrug. "I imagine Gloria is simply jealous of you."

"Jealous?" both Marie and I asked in unison.

"Gloria wants nothing to do with any of these crimes," Marie said.

"Maybe not the crimes, but the attention that involvement could bring," Felix said. "Not to mention the fact that Lillian has Mr. Osbourn, and a suitor is something that Gloria wants for herself."

I looked over at Marie, watching her face. The way her eyebrows rose was all the confirmation I needed.

"This reminds me that I need to speak with Richard about something..." I said. "However, *that* will have to wait. For now, I think we should consider where we ought to meet this new potential client of ours."

"Of course," Felix said. "What say you, William? Any suggestions of a quiet public park where we could meet our new friend?"

"Oh, I know the perfect place," William said, brightening. "Here, let me show you."

It seemed we were about to begin our new adventure and our first official case as detectives for hire.

3

"Well, I'll give the boy one thing," Felix said, looking around. "He certainly knew exactly what we meant when we said *quiet*."

The park that William had suggested was situated in one of the nicest neighborhoods in the heart of London. Often passed over for the bigger and more open parks like Hyde or St. James's, it was evidently a bit of a secret among those who sought peace in the midst of the city life. It did not have many ponds or large open spaces, but felt vaguely like a forest glade one might find at the edge of a country estate.

Somehow, the sounds of the city seemed to fade away as soon as we passed through the gates into the park proper. It was one of the first days in almost three weeks that the entire city and its surrounding suburbs were not being pounded with rain.

"Yes, for a ten-year-old William understands the importance of keeping things discreet," I said as we followed the somewhat sodden path toward the center of the park. "Seriously, if we continue this business, if he is still interested when he turns eighteen, we could hire him on as a freelancer."

"I rather like the idea," Felix said. "Oh, watch the puddles. I wouldn't want you to ruin your new shoes."

"Thank you," I said, taking his hand, as he helped me to hop over a particularly wide pool that stretched all the way across the dirt path. "Now...if our new client received our letter, then we should be able to spot him or her."

"Most likely a woman," my brother said. "The penmanship seemed feminine."

I didn't disagree.

"I have been thinking about this," Felix continued, gazing around the park, his steely blue eyes narrowing sharply. "What sort person do you expect to meet?"

I looked up at him, the wind beginning to pick up, swirling some of my hair around my eyes. I pushed it back behind my ears, gazing up at the darkening sky. Would we really have to endure rain again? It made me miss the old New York summers, which were the most beautiful season we had. "Playing this game again, are we?" I asked with a smirk.

"Do you remember that night when we were eight or nine, and Mother and Father were giving that dinner for the children's hospital? She talked about that Mr. Walters for days and days, and all we could think was that he looked like a walrus?"

I laughed. "That's the very same memory I thought of," I said. "Or that dinner when we sat up in the balcony over the ballroom, watching the guests and discussing who they might have been, and the ridiculous lives they had?"

"Such as the woman with the large, feathered hat, who we swore bred peacocks for circuses," Felix said.

"Or that fellow with the fur coat, who we assumed came all the way from Siberia to raise sled dogs," I said.

We shared a moment of laughter together, and it made me entirely forget the real reason we were there at the park, waiting.

When the realization hit me, my smile faded ever so slightly. "...My word. How quickly time has gone."

Felix seemed sober, as well, and stared off into the distance.

We continued to walk down the path, glancing between the trees for the benches scattered around. Most were empty, indicating the park was as private as William had said it would be.

We spotted one bench that was occupied, though... and it held a woman wearing a blue hat, tossing small handfuls of breadcrumbs down to the ducks wandering along the path.

I gave Felix a tap on the arm, and he followed my subtle gesture in her direction.

He turned to look both up and down the path; I followed suit, and it seemed that we were alone. We had seen a few other people in the park, but it had only been a young family with their children, and an elderly couple strolling through, hand in hand.

Felix and I tried to be as casual as we could, drawing nearer to the woman. It was entirely possible that her presence was nothing more than coincidence. Obviously, there had to be more than one person in all of London who owned a blue hat, though the shade of this one was a little unique.

We were coming up on her, and I looked down at her just as she looked up at me.

It was then that I realized she wore a mesh veil over her face that was attached to her hat, as if in mourning.

Quickly, we assessed one another with nothing more than a glance. It was not long before her whole body stiffened, and she said, "You are the ones, aren't you?"

Her voice sounded familiar, though I could not immediately place it.

Felix slowed beside me as I turned to her. "Yes, indeed we are," I said. "And you must be the anonymous writer of the letter we received."

I could just make out the woman's eyes through the veil, as her gaze passed over me as if discerning whether we were speaking of the same matters. "What is your surname?"

"Crawford," I said. "And yes, we are the ones who put the advertisement in the paper."

She let out a long sigh of relief, laying a hand over her heart. "I was beginning to think I had been a bit too presumptuous to write in the first place, wondering if I had simply been overreacting."

"I suppose we won't know until we have a chance to speak," I said. "Though I imagine it must be an important matter for you to have contacted us."

She hesitated for a moment. "Would you care to sit with me?" she asked, moving all the way down to the end of the bench.

I sat beside her, and Felix beside me.

The woman tossed the rest of her bread onto the

ground, and the ducks seemed all too keen to gobble it up with a quiet chorus of *quack, quack, quack* amongst themselves.

"Were you followed?" she asked in a low voice, her head turning as she gazed up the length of the path.

"No," I said.

"Not as far as we know, anyway," Felix said. "Your note did not mention that we should expect to be."

"Did anyone know you were coming?" she asked.

"No one apart from a few members of our family that we are currently residing with," I said. "Why?"

"I do not wish anyone to know we are meeting here," she said. "I'm worried about how far these people will go, how long their reach has become."

"I am sorry you have been so tormented," Felix said. "Why don't you tell us what has been happening?"

"And your name, if you feel comfortable enough," I said. "Along with a moment to see your face. I know you wished to keep you anonymity, but we may not be able to help you if we don't know who it is we are trying to help."

"My face?" she asked.

"I am not a fool, ma'am. I like to look my clients in the eye in order to discern if they are telling me the truth. Surely, you can understand."

She hesitated even longer. "Very well," she said. "Though I only attached the veil so no one would recognize me."

"Something that makes perfect sense," I said. "But you must understand why we need to see you. What if someone was impersonating you? Or we meet someone later who claims to be you? How could we know otherwise?"

She slowly reached up and unhooked the veil from inside the hat. She let it fall to her shoulder.

She was a pretty woman, perhaps a decade older than Felix and I, and retaining many youthful features. Her hair, a brilliant blonde, had been pinned up in a sweeping fashion around the back of her head. I might not have picked her out of a crowd, as ordinary as she seemed, but she wore an interesting copper necklace with a pendent in the shape of a small spyglass, which hung to her collarbone over the top of her high-collared, blue dress.

Her expression nervous, she smoothed her hands over her skirts, and pursed her lips. "And...my name is Mrs. Carter."

"Well, it is a pleasure to meet you, Mrs. Carter," I said. "My name is Miss Lillian Crawford, and this is my brother, Mr. Felix Crawford. Thank you for honoring our request."

"How do you do, ma'am?" Felix asked.

She gave us an uneasy smile. "Thank you for answering my letter," she said.

I snapped my fingers, which made both her and Felix jump on either side of me. I looked at her. "Now I remember!" I said. "I thought I recognized your voice. We've met before, haven't we?"

She flushed, and looked away. "I had wondered if you would remember me," she said.

"You were at a Mr. Culpepper's funeral, which we attended not long ago," I said.

She nodded.

"Oh, that's right," Felix said. "I thought I recognized you as well. Is that how you learned about us?"

"Yes," she said. "I heard about the pair of detectives who came through to help that family when they suspected Mr. Culpepper had been murdered, and his sister spoke quite highly of you. At the time, I found it rather fascinating, but then as soon as the troubles began in my own family, I thought about reaching out to her for more information, including how I might be able to get in touch with you."

I frowned. "So you did not see our advertisement in the paper, then?"

"I did," she said. "That is what pushed me to contact you. It seemed as if destiny itself had reached out to give me a sign that I needed."

The elderly couple had found their way to the side of the park where we were all sitting, and Mrs. Carter spotted them. She gave a small gasp, and her hands jumped to her veil, quickly reattaching it to her hat.

"I suppose word of mouth is just as good as the newspaper," I said. "I am pleased to hear that Mr. Culpepper's sister was as satisfied with our work as she was." I did my best to keep our conversation inane, so as not to draw attention to it by the couple. It was unlikely that they were anyone of concern, but with as little as we knew about her circumstances, it was better to err on the side of caution.

"Yes, she was very pleased...well, as pleased as one might be with the reasons as to why she called you in the first place," she said.

The couple continued to plod along the path, drawing nearer. They were surely within earshot by now, so we would have to put the real reason for our conversation on hold.

"I must ask you, Mrs. Carter, about the necklace..." I said, gesturing to it hanging from her neck. "I have never seen such an interesting piece."

She reached up to touch it, almost without thought. "A gift from my husband many years ago," she said. "Just before we were married. It was his way of telling me that no matter what happened, he would always keep his focus upon me, and eventually, our family if we had children...which we do now, five of them."

"How thoughtful of him," I remarked, watching the elderly couple continue on up the path.

The three of us waited a few more minutes, until they were far enough away that we could be certain they would not be able to overhear anything we would say.

"I fear we do not have much time," Mrs. Carter said. "What with these interruptions."

"Very well, then let us get right down to the point," I said. "Tell us what it is that you need us to do."

"First, we would like to know who has died," Felix said.

"Yes," I said. "That would be the best place to start, I think."

"No one has died," Mrs. Carter said, a slight tremble in her voice. "But I fear that is what may happen."

This seemed more and more worthwhile of a visit the longer we spoke with her.

"I am...I am beside myself with worry," she said, and her voice cracked as if fighting back tears. "I have nowhere else to turn. My husband...I believe he is in great danger, but no one seems to be taking my fears seriously."

"Why not?" I asked. The wind had picked up, swirling around the bench, causing leaves to dance over our feet.

"I don't know," she said, shaking her head. "My husband believes I am being far too paranoid, but I think he is being foolish by refusing to take any sort of precaution. He does not believe himself to be in any real danger, you see."

"Any *real* danger?" I emphasized.

"Yes," she said. "We have been receiving threat after threat, and my husband thinks them to be nothing more than a bluff."

"What sort of threats?" Felix asked.

"They started small," Mrs. Carter said. "I might have even said harmless at the time. My husband is the owner of a rather large business, after all. There have always been those who are jealous of his success, who want it for themselves and have been quite open about it...but this all felt...different, somehow."

"What's happened?" I asked.

"We began to receive letters at our home address, which is rare, as my husband is very private about our family. They all have been in a strange hand that we do not recognize, and I do mean strange. It is almost as if they were all written...upside down, or perhaps with a non-dominant hand, but they look as though a child has written them. Some were nearly indiscernible."

"What did these letters say?" Felix asked.

She said, "They began as subtle threats, such as warning my husband to sign off on a certain policy, or not to go forward with the hiring or dismissing of a particular manager. He told me these were the sorts of 'complaint' letters he received regularly at his office, where he welcomed scrutiny and criticism as a means of keeping himself accountable to both his employees and the public. But then...they became more extreme. Wishing harm upon him, and his family, or warning him that he would regret his decisions. All ominous, and all terrifying."

She laid a hand over her heart once more, and I could see the quick, shallow gasps that she drew in.

"It's all right," I told her, trying to put her at ease by laying my hand on her arm. "We are going to help you."

She took in a deeper, shakier breath. She turned her face back toward me, and though I could not see her eyes, I could feel her gaze upon me. "That isn't the end of it," she said. "The threats grew more severe. One morning when taking my youngest two children out for a walk, I noticed that one of my prized rose bushes in the side garden had been destroyed, cut all the way down to the roots."

"That's quite disturbing," Felix said.

"That is precisely what I thought, as well," Mrs. Carter said. "Then my older three children were followed home from an outing with their nanny. They told me that a strange man had started after them, and always stayed at a distance but never veered away, continuing along the exact same path they did."

"How dreadful," I said.

"The most recent event happened not even a week ago, when a brick was thrown through the window of our dining room. Thankfully we weren't home at the time, but when we returned, our butler showed us the brick with a note attached, which simply told my husband that if he did not refrain from his doings, there would be more severe repercussions."

My brows rose, and I gave Felix a sidelong glance.

He, too, seemed concerned.

This might have been one of the more startling cases we had taken on thus far.

"Well, it certainly seems as if you are right in trying to take precautions," I said. "Though you say that your husband does not agree?"

"He does not believe it necessary," she said with a shrug. "I have expressed clearly that we should be taking this much more seriously, but he simply refuses to listen to me."

"Not to veer too far from the subject, ma'am, but what is your husband doing that is drawing these sorts of threats?" Felix asked, leaning over to rest his elbows upon his knees.

She gave a great sigh, and folded her hands in her lap. "He is the head of a large company here in town," she said. "Naturally, as I said earlier, there will always be naysayers."

"Of course," I said. "That is to be expected of anyone in a leadership position."

"My husband, unlike many who would typically be in his position, does not bend to the whims and desires of all the board members and major share holders," she said. "He makes a great many unpopular decisions, being a staunch believer in doing everything above board, rather than always acting to line the pockets of his business associates. As one might imagine, there are those who do not take kindly to that way of thinking."

"No, I can imagine not..." I said.

"We do have a better understanding than you might realize, ma'am," Felix said. "Our father is one of the top financial advisors in New York, you see. We understand what it is like to rub shoulders with the sorts of men that are against your husband."

I crossed my arms. "Which is why I must know if your husband truly is trustworthy," I said, my eyes narrowing. "If *you* are trustworthy. How can we be certain that you are not simply trying to fool us to some degree?"

"Oh, I can assure you I am doing no such thing," she said. "As I said, I am coming to you out of the fear and sickness in my heart. My husband knows these men he works with are snakes, that they will go to great lengths to protect their wealth and reputations, but he does not think they would ever truly do anything to harm him or his family, given all the good he has brought to the company. He tries to assure me these men won't do anything to 'bite the hand that feeds them', as he says."

"Yes, but what if all they have to do is replace the one that does just that?" I asked.

She nodded fervently, her hat bobbing. "That is *precisely* my point," she said. "He tells me they never would, that they respect him far too much, but I believe they would think nothing of removing him if it was for their own betterment."

I looked at Felix, whose brow had furrowed. I could see the wheels turning behind his eyes as he tugged on the end of his earlobe, an action I had not seen him do in some time.

"This seems to be the perfect job for us, doesn't it, Lil?" he asked a few moments later. "Who else is better suited to investigate millionaires and shady businessmen than we?"

"I can think of no one," I said, turning back to Mrs. Carter. "I can certainly see why you are worried. I will not waste your time with tales of our own experiences, but rest assured, we know how ugly these sorts of people can be when crossed."

"It's good that you decided to come to us now, and not after...well, after things grew worse," Felix put in.

I did not want to think about what worse might look like, and I imagined neither did Mrs. Carter.

"My husband is stubborn, even as good natured as he is," Mrs. Carter said, her voice thick with tears not far behind. "But I worry about how far these people might go, and what that could mean for our family. I'm terrified of my children having to endure some horrific act because their father would not seek outside help, believing he could do it all on his own when he does not have to."

I looked back over at Felix, who gave me a nod. He was ready. He even seemed steady, confident. It gave me hope.

"We would be glad to take your case, Mrs. Carter," I said. "We – "

A roll of thunder in the distance caused all three of us to turn and look toward the south. Shadows permeated the clouds, hiding away what little sunlight must have been trying to break through. It made me wonder when I had last seen the blue of the sky.

"Another storm," Felix said in a low voice.

"How fitting," I said. "Well, before this storm reaches us, let us deal with the situation at hand. We will of course help you, and will do all we can to intercede on your family's behalf."

"Thank you..." she said. "And...you two said that your father works in finance in New York?"

"That's right," Felix said.

"Which means that you both must come from a rather wealthy family then, yes?"

"We do," I said. "Why do you ask?"

Mrs. Carter paused, and glanced out over the park. "I've had an idea, and it just might work."

"Oh?" I asked, a small smile stretching across my face. "What sort of an idea?"

She bent her head in closer to us. "This is what I am thinking..."

As we began our plotting, the storm continued rumbling ominously overhead.

4

Heavy droplets of rain as large as marbles pelted the top of the car, in such a thick sheet that I could hardly see the streetlamps along the road.

"It's a wonder the whole roof hasn't caved in yet," Felix said with a small chuckle, and still checking with a glance upward all the same.

I smoothed my coat, wondering if it would be sufficient to protect my sequined evening gown and the feathered ruff at my neck when next we got out of the car. Even my cap of dark hair, carefully arranged to hug my skull beneath a beaded headband, would likely get a soaking.

"If I didn't know better, I would think we were in the midst of a hurricane," I said in a scathing tone, leaning forward to try and make sense of what lay ahead of us through the windshield.

"Oh, I've seen worse," said Ronald, the chauffeur in

the front seat. "Hopefully this car will be moving in a moment."

We had been no more than three or four miles from the Carter residence when we had reached a backed up street, which according to Ronald was caused by a car that had broken down in the middle of an intersection up ahead. By the time we had realized we were stuck, we couldn't turn around due to all the traffic behind us.

I let out a groan and sank back against the seat, shaking my head. "We are going to be late."

"Consider it a mark of superiority, sister," Felix said. "Everyone will wonder what is so special about the pair of us that we have deemed it acceptable to show up whenever we please."

"Right you are," Ronald said with a chuckle. "I am sorry about the delay, though. I'll get you there as soon as I'm able."

"It's not your fault," I said heavily, though I couldn't help but feel a bit frustrated that he chose this direction to go; he was the one driving, after all.

"Part of it's the blasted rain," Ronald went on, gripping the steering wheel as he tried to look up at the sky through the windshield. "Once it lets up, people will feel better about going through it. Right now, we can hardly see the vehicle in front of us."

"I suppose we can use the time to go over the plan for the night again," Felix said to me.

"Felix, we have done this three times," I said, glaring at him.

"Do you have any better suggestions as to how we should pass the time right now?" Felix asked, arching a brow. "Anything else that might be more productive?"

I groaned, rolling my eyes. "Fine," I said. "Fine. What do you want to review?"

"The dinner tonight is for the partners of Mr. Carter's company," Felix said, pulling a piece of paper from his pocket and unfolding it. "Mrs. Carter said there might also be some personal friends of her husband who have connections to his company."

"The point of the dinner is to try and convince the other heads of the company of Mr. Carter's newest idea, which is to make some changes with the finances, which will be good for employees but costly in the short term," I said. I looked up at Felix. "It seems as if none of them want to go for the plan."

"Exactly," Felix said. He ran his thumb over the paper, smoothing some of the creases. "Now, our story...we are attending under the rouse that we are new friends of Mrs. Carter."

"Yes, and that the Carters met us at a charity dinner a few weeks ago," I said, reading my brother's notes over his shoulder, which was nearly impossible in the dimness of the car. It seemed as if the rain was somehow drowning out the bright light of the nearby windows and street-lamps. I shook my head, trying to see *something* through the torrential downpour ahead of us. "Mrs. Carter has assured us her husband will simply believe what she says, but much of our plan will be foiled if, for some reason, he does not."

"I think she knows him well enough to know what he will be willing to accept," Felix said.

"From the sounds of it, he's a busy man," Ronald said with a glance in the rearview mirror. "If he is the head of one of the biggest businesses in London, it's very likely he meets more people than he is ever able to remember."

"That's probably true," Felix said. "We could have actually met Mr. Carter a time or two and he would still have forgotten us."

I crossed my arms. "Would he really forget the children of a New York millionaire?" I asked.

"Maybe not, but I think for our purposes this evening, he will accept his wife's words," Felix said.

"You mean her lies," I said.

Felix shrugged. "Then I suppose it's good we are getting our story straight, isn't it?" He returned his eyes to the paper. "Oh, yes...Mrs. Carter also said she believes Mr. Carter wishes to bring all these men together as a means of proving her worries wrong, a chance to air the troubles between them all."

"I still think it would be incredibly unwise for him to bring up the threats they've been receiving," I said. "What if it pushes the person sending them to escalate from threats to planning some physical attack against Mr. Carter? Or his wife?"

Felix nodded. "I believe that's part of the reason she has invited us to attend this dinner in particular, as if I recall correctly, Mrs. Carter mentioned that Mr. Carter intends on giving them all a chance to come clean."

My brow furrowed. "Is he a complete and utter fool?" I asked.

Felix shook his head. "I doubt he is that unthinking, but it certainly seems as if he might underestimate those he is inviting into his home. Unless, of course, he is far cleverer than we realize and is already expecting them to react poorly. Playing chess a few steps ahead, if you will."

I considered for a moment, watching the car in front of us begin to slowly move forward, braving the rain. "That would make sense, I suppose," I said. "One does not acquire a position as important as his by chance."

"True," Felix agreed. "Perhaps we would be wise not to underestimate Mr. Carter."

"Anyway, more than anything, I think his wife is hoping we will get a feel for these men," I said. "It is quite unlikely we will be able to discern who has been sending the threats tonight, but at least we might find a lead or two."

"Correct," Felix said. "It will be good to have the chance to look them in the eye and see which ones flinch."

I grinned. "This case was made for us, Felix. They won't even know what hit them."

His smile grew, too.

"Good news," Ronald said as the engine revved back to life. "We have movement ahead!"

To my great relief, the rain eased up enough for Ronald to be able to navigate around the stalled car in the intersection. It was slow going, but if not for the police standing out in the middle, rain streaming from the brims of their hats like waterfalls, there might have been more accidents than had already occurred. Ronald remained patient, humming all the while he drove us down the narrow, busy streets.

"It seems everyone is hoping to get out of the rain," Felix said, staring through the sheets of water cascading down the window glass.

"Or they have chosen this as the best possible time to go out and attend an elaborate dinner party or some such," I said. I chuckled. "I mean, who are we, but those going to some party that is entirely unnecessary in this weather?"

"It just means we are dedicated," Felix said.

"That, and trouble is afoot," I said.

"I apologize for the interruption, but I don't know how familiar the both of you are with London," Ronald said with a quick glance over his shoulder as we made a left turn at the end of the street. "It might be rather dreary today, but this is the famous Hyde Park."

He gestured toward one side of the car, and Felix and I both gazed out through the dark, grey night. Seeing the bleary lights that lined the pathway into the park, my spirits rose.

"Mr. Carter lives near the park? My, we are dining with important people then, aren't we?" I said. "There is something enchanting about being in the heart of London."

"It makes me miss New York, in a small way," Felix said.

I wrinkled my nose. "Not *me*. If I never stepped foot back in New York, I think it would be too soon."

Felix turned to look at me as Hyde Park disappeared out through the back window. "Really? I thought you would have missed it at least somewhat."

I shook my head. "I would be very pleased if I never went back."

Felix considered for a moment, and I could see the wheels turning in his mind. "Well, that certainly surprises me. I've missed several aspects of life back home."

I shrugged. "I suppose homesickness has come and

gone for me, but...there is so much of England that I have not seen."

"What of our parents?" Felix asked.

I let out a groan. "I don't think they would care if I ever returned," I said. "In all of Mother's letters, she is short and distant. I don't think she misses me at all."

Felix frowned. "I doubt that's true."

"Well...maybe not, but as of right now, I think I will remain around London for as long as Cousin Richard will have me," I said.

Felix nodded. "I suppose you will want to wait and see what happens with Mr. Osbourn, yes?"

My face colored, and I looked away. "Eugene Osbourn can do as he pleases," I said, folding my arms.

"As long as it's marry you, right?" Felix teased.

I glared at him as the car came to a stop. In truth, I had not even heard from Eugene in some time, and was beginning to wonder why.

"Here we are," Ronald said.

I looked out the window up at the white-fronted rowhouse. It was incredibly difficult to see through the trails of rain running like small rivers down the window. I only got a good, clear view once we were standing on the sidewalk, Felix holding an umbrella over our heads. It was a beautiful home, with marble pillars and gold details in the corners of the windows. Everything was clean, looking as though it was maintained on a regular basis, including the flower boxes and the burgundy paint on the front door.

"I'll remain here," Ronald said as he closed the car door behind us, squinting as rain pelted his cheeks. "No sense in driving all the way back to Mr. Sansbury's. Might not get that far, anyway."

"You really are going to stay out in this rain?" I asked.

"The whole city is going to be crawling like a snail on its belly with this weather," Ronald said, pointing up toward the pregnant clouds. "I am happy to wait as long as needed."

"Very well..." I said. "Try not to drown, will you?"

He grinned. "I'm practically a fish, Miss. Hardly a chance."

He hurried around the other side of the car, and got himself tucked away inside.

"He'll be fine," Felix said. "Come on. Let's not delay any longer."

We made our way to the front door, where we only had to wait a few heartbeats before our knocking was answered. A handsome butler greeted us, much younger than many of the butlers we had met. "Good evening. Please step inside."

"Thank you," Felix said, leading me in through the door.

Glancing around, I quickly noted that our hosts favored a traditional, old fashioned style of décor with tarnished gold, gilded mirrors, and tufted silk chairs with their original pearl buttons. There were also polished wooden tables with elegant legs adorned with carvings in the shapes of ivy and flowers. It seemed a delicate style, likely born of inspiration from the countryside.

"My name is Mr. Lewis, but you may simply refer to me as Lewis during your time here," the butler said, smoothly closing the door behind us. "Might I take your umbrella and coats?"

"Of course," Felix said, allowing Lewis to do just that.

"I hope we aren't too late," I said, slithering out of my own damp coat as well.

"Not at all," Lewis said. "Many of the guests have had trouble arriving this evening, with the rain as bad as it has been."

"Is the summer always so...drenched?" I asked.

Lewis gave us a small smile. "I assume you have not been in London long?" he asked. "No, this is a bit abnormal. Rain is to be expected, and grey skies are often the usual sight, but this amount of rain? No, this is unusual."

"The roads were quite treacherous, as well," Felix said.

"As we have heard," Lewis said. "One of the guests, Mr. Lee, said that he nearly slipped down his own front stairs due to the amount of water pouring down the steps."

"My goodness," I said. "It's a shock the whole city isn't underwater yet."

"And that is how some say the ancient city of Atlantis disappeared," said a voice across the foyer.

I turned to see a man striding into the room, with Mrs. Carter on his arm.

"Ah, Mr. Carter," Felix said, holding his hand out to the man as they approached. "How nice to see you again, sir."

Mr. Carter smiled at him, but I could see the slight twinge of his brow; he did not recognize us.

Naturally, as we've never met him.

He was a good compliment to his wife, as handsome as she was lovely. His dark hair, peppered with grey along his temples, was cut close to his head. He sported a beard, also closely trimmed, grey marbling through. He had bright blue eyes and was dressed well, clean and sleek.

Mrs. Carter wore a lovely, pale blue gown with heavy beading around the scooped neck, and had a shawl of some wispy, sheer fabric draped loosely over her arms. Without the hat and veil, she was radiant. She smiled at us, and I could see the reminder in her eyes; *Don't tell him.*

Not to worry, Mrs. Carter. Our lips are sealed. Prepare to be amazed. You will not regret your decision to hire us.

"Yes, it is nice to see you, as well..." Mr. Carter said. He shook Felix's hand. "Welcome to our humble home."

The description of this extravagant house as humble made my lips twitch, but I hid my amusement.

"Thank you sir, we are pleased to be here," Felix said.

"Yes, thank you again for having us this evening," I said, giving Mrs. Carter a broad smile.

She returned it easily. The relief was already palpable in her expression.

"You will have to forgive me, my dear, but I am having trouble remembering precisely who these fine people are," Mr. Carter said, laying a hand atop that of his wife, looking at Felix and me out of the corner of his eye.

"Oh, darling, how could you have forgotten?" she asked. "We met them just two weeks ago at the charity dinner for the hospital."

Mr. Carter snapped his fingers. "Oh, yes, that's right. Now I remember," he said, beaming at the pair of us. "This is...?"

"Mr. Felix Crawford, and my sister, Miss Lillian Crawford," Felix said, indicating the pair of us.

Mr. Carter's brows wrinkled. "You are siblings, I take it?"

"I am pleased you were able to deduce that; not long ago, my brother and I were mistaken for a quarreling, loveless couple," I said.

Mr. Carter laughed. "You are joking?"

"Not at all," Felix said, smoothly picking up my fib. "A gentleman asked just what I had done to distress my wife so much, to which I replied that he would have to be more specific, as I had not been informed that I was married in the first place."

Mr. and Mrs. Carter both laughed, and I gave Felix an appreciative grin. I could always count on him to master-fully follow the flow of the conversation I was trying to steer, and make it seem entirely natural.

"How could I have forgotten you?" Mr. Carter asked, clapping Felix on the shoulder. "Your sense of humor will be welcome this evening, as some of our other guests are a bit...chilly."

"Well, we will just have to change that," I said.

"I would appreciate it," Mr. Carter said. "Again, I do apologize. There have been several times over the past few years when I have been introduced to people that I later simply cannot remember."

"Well, you do meet a great many people, Mr. Carter," I said, charitably. "I imagine it would be terribly difficult to remember them all."

"You are too kind," he said, and it seemed that I had won some favor with him, judging by his nervous smile.

It certainly seemed that Mrs. Carter had been correct about her husband, and his acceptance of our presence in their home. He didn't question it, though I had worried he might when he had first seen us. Thankfully, Felix and

I had appeared good-natured enough, and given his own character, he warmed to us easily.

If I felt guilty, it was only a little, and the feeling vanished quickly. We were here to help this man and to protect his family, after all.

"We are just going to wait for the last of the guests to arrive," Mrs. Carter said. "If you two so desire, you may go on ahead to the drawing room where everyone else is waiting."

"Yes, and dinner should be ready soon enough," Mr. Carter said. "Lewis will show you the way."

We followed Lewis down the hall, and up a small flight of four stairs to another hall with a room on either side, where through the one on the left the sounds of conversation and laughter could be heard.

"Here you are," Lewis said. "I will come and announce when it is time for dinner."

Felix nodded, and he held out his arm to me so that we could enter the room together.

The drawing room seemed just as luxurious as the foyer, with dark, rich wooden shelves lining both the north and south walls, and floor to ceiling windows draped in thick, velvet curtains along the far western wall. It smelled of cigars and roses, and I noticed vases on nearly every surface filled with stunning pink roses. *Those must be from Mrs. Carter's prized rose bushes.*

I took a quick look around the room. I seemed to be the only woman in attendance, as all I could see were men, three of whom had gathered near the far windows. Two others lingered near the fireplace, and a solitary man stood examining the bookshelves –

I prodded Felix in the forearm, and he looked down. "Hmm?"

"That man…" I said, eyes squinting. "The bald one, near the shelves. Why does he look so familiar?"

Felix turned his head, and then his eyes widened with recognition.

"Who is it?" I asked.

"Mr. McDonough," Felix said, his mouth hanging slightly open.

"Mr. McDonough?" I repeated. "What is he doing here?"

Our entrance had drawn the attention of some of the other guests, all of whom looked at us with varying degrees of scrutiny. That was of little surprise, given that not one of them would have recognized us. Well…none but one.

Mr. Charles McDonough, likely feeling a shift in the atmosphere of the room, glanced over his shoulder and spotted us just inside the doorway. His gaze sharpened at once, yet apart from the somewhat disgruntled expressions, his movement toward us did not seem to garner any question from anyone else.

Felix and I met him near a card table that had been neatly stacked with various decks of cards, three of which seemed to be in different languages.

"Mr. and Miss Crawford," he said in that deep, silky voice of his. His brow furrowed, his bald head glistening like a freshly polished marble statue in the warm light of the room. "What a surprise it is to see you here, of all places."

"It is hardly a shock that we might cross paths at *some* point, Mr. McDonough," I said. "This city might be large, but there are only so many families in our unique...situation." That of being in possession of great amounts of wealth and status, I meant. He, like our father, was an important man back in New York, and it was that slight acquaintance that had led to our spending some time with he and his wife on the boat over to England.

Mr. McDonough's shoulders rolled uncomfortably, and he took a look around at the other guests in the room. Only one man shot a quick glance in our direction, with as scrutinizing of a gaze as I might have expected.

Ah...it seems that I am home once again.

These were the sorts of looks I was used to, that I had grown up around. A smile that spelled hatred, a glance that made an important decision, a laugh that held more malice than warmth. I understood them for the language they were; the language of the rich and the elite.

"You might reconsider being so open with your family's economic situation," Mr. McDonough said in a low voice. "I cannot imagine your father would fancy hearing you be so flippant."

My gaze hardened. "We are all from the same place, Mr. McDonough. They are going to know that we must be connected in some way, attending the same party as we are."

"Yes, and why hide how we are acquainted?" Felix added. "When those of the same standing in New York would have known it before they had even laid eyes on us?"

Mr. McDonough's eyes flashed. "We are not *in* New York, are we?" he asked in a low voice, his gaze passing over the room once again. "These men...they operate in a different way than those we might know. They already care little for me because I am an American."

I smirked, watching him. It could not have been more obvious that our presence had entirely caught him off guard.

"If we are to share the same room for the evening, then let us clear the air between us," Mr. McDonough said, his large forehead furrowing. "Despite everything that happened when we were on the ship together, and although I do not appreciate being falsely accused as I was, I must commend you for solving that case before anything worse occurred."

My pride swelled a bit, and my smile grew. "Thank you, Mr. McDonough," I said.

He continued, "All the same, I find it strange that we should meet again, and so I must ask...what are the two of you doing here?"

"I was about to ask you the very same question, Mr. McDonough," Felix said. "How are you acquainted with the Carters?"

"Mr. Carter and I are old friends," Mr. McDonough said easily. I knew at once that he was not lying, as his gaze was steady, his voice not wavering in the slightest. "He and I have been speaking over the past few years about some of the policies he wishes to put into place at his company, and I have come over to help him draw them up."

"You are familiar with the workings of the business?" Felix asked.

"In a small way, yes," Mr. McDonough said. "I do not have my hand in quite so many pies as Mr. Carter, but I am familiar with the way that he leads, as his style is similar to my own."

"Father has always told me of your rather unorthodox business practices," Felix said. "He said that you were ruthless, but merciful."

Mr. McDonough arched a brow. "Leave it to your father to describe me as ruthless. You must not believe everything you hear."

"You said Mr. Carter wanted your help?" I prompted.

"Well, my help and support," Mr. McDonough said. "I am perhaps one of the few businessmen who would support his decision, given the money to be sacrificed in the short term. He is about to take an unpopular stance that would be expensive for the company partners but would benefit lower level employees, and would be good for the whole company over time. Unsurprisingly, his business associates are opposed to his idea, but this dinner is to be a means of changing their minds. That is the hope, anyway."

"It does not seem that either Mr. Carter or his wife believe the occasion is going to go over well," I said.

"It may not," Mr. McDonough said. "It all depends on whether the attendees are willing to listen to reason."

I am starting to believe Mrs. Carter's worries are not unfounded.

"Have you heard of the threats Mr. Carter has been receiving?" Felix asked.

I shot him a look out of the corner of my eye. How could he be so sure we could trust Mr. McDonough? Yes, we might know him well enough, but did that mean he would be on our side? His story might sound convincing, but was it wise to bring all this right out in the open? *I*

thought we had agreed we were not going to reveal our inten-
tions to anyone here this evening, so that we could observe
without scrutiny?

"Yes, I have heard..." Mr. McDonough said with a
heaviness in his words that surprised me. "It concerns
me, but he does not seem troubled by them."

"Mrs. Carter is worried," I said. "She has expressed
that to us several times."

Mr. McDonough's eyes flashed again. "You seem very
interested in the company and Mr. Carter's part in it, yet
you have not shared with me why you happen to be here
the same evening I am. I have never heard Mr. Carter
speak your names, so you must forgive me for
wondering."

"We came at Mrs. Carter's request," I said. "We met
recently, having been connected through a mutual
acquaintance –"

A bell sounded near the door, a pleasant chime that
cut through the droll voices. I breathed a private sigh of
relief. I did not quite know where Mr. McDonough would
carry the conversation, but for the time being it seemed
as if Felix and I would keep our secret...at least until we
needed to do otherwise.

5

The poached quail with rosemary potatoes and a hearty serving of trifle with delectable clotted cream might have been delicious beyond measure, prepared with great care and skill...but poor company soured the whole meal all together.

I glared across the table at the pair of men who threw back their heads and laughed yet again at the expense of a rather unfortunate priest who they claimed brayed like a donkey whenever he would sing. Childish, derisive humor against one who was not present to defend himself, yet they seemed to know no other form. They were named Mr. Turner and Mr. Lee.

I groaned as I shot Felix a disgruntled look, skimming my spoon along the bottom of my trifle. I'd lost my appetite for the last few bites after Mr. Lee made a remark about how amusing it was when his younger brother had fallen down the stairs and broken his leg just a few weeks before. All he seemed to consider was the cost, thankful that he didn't have to pay the doctor as much as his brother in order to set the bone.

Mr. Lee seemed to be one of the more prominent partners in the company, second only to Mr. Ward, who was directly beneath Mr. Carter in standing.

It was becoming increasingly clear that Mrs. Carter and Mr. McDonough's concerns were well founded. These men had little regard for Mr. Carter or his family, either making rude jokes at his expense, or ignoring what he said entirely. Mr. Turner laughed at the way his hair was cut like a school child right after Mr. Ward chided him for providing what he considered to be a lackluster quail.

My nose wrinkled as Mr. Lee let out another guffaw of laughter, and the sound nearly made me drop my spoon. I tensed, clenching my fist around the silver.

Felix gave me a nudge with the tip of his shoe, and I glanced sidelong to see him staring at me with a quick, furrowed brow of warning. We were there to observe, his look reminded me. The table manners of our fellow guests were not important.

He was right, of course, but that did not make it easy to stomach the obnoxious way these men spoke and acted.

They all even look somewhat alike.

All except for Mr. Carter, that was. Each of them had a variation of a portly belly, some more protruding than others. Mr. Lee had quite a bit of hair atop his head, but it was thinning near his hairline. The others all had thinning hair or were entirely bald like Mr. Ward. Each male guest wore unvarying dark dinner jackets paired with stiff, white collars and waistcoats.

Maybe their similar educations and careers made it easy for them to all turn out the same, dress the same, and behave the same.

I glanced up the table at Mrs. Carter, who sat beside her husband, patiently attempting to engage the nearest guest in conversation. But that guest, a Mr. Clayton, seemed far more interested in the joking that was taking place further up the table.

My attention was drawn from the group, when the hairs on the back of my neck began to stand straight, as I sensed eyes on me. I looked around to find precisely where the gaze I felt was coming from. With a small skip of my heart, I found it almost at once...and it was Mr. Lee who was sitting directly across from me.

I met his stare, and as soon as I noticed him, the rather nasty sneer fixed to his face grew wider. He was not at all what one might consider handsome, reminding me more of a weasel or a rat with his pointed nose, beady eyes, and a large mole along his jawline. His eyebrows rose repeatedly in what I could only assume was a suggestive fashion.

In the right circumstances, it might have been humorous, but considering the source, I had to resist the urge to grimace at him.

I needed a distraction, or I would lose my temper and draw excessive attention from our fellow guests.

I swept the back of my hand over the fork resting on the table, and it slid off the edge, clattering down onto the floor between Felix and me.

At once, I bent over to fetch it at the same time that Felix happened to reach for it.

"Mr. Lee is staring at me," I hissed under my breath as I fumbled around on the floor for the fork.

"I've noticed," Felix said.

"I don't like it," I grumbled.

"Nor I," Felix said. "But we must maintain appearances."

"Yes, I realize that, but I am unhappy about it all," I said.

"We need to take care, as from what I have deduced, Mr. Lee is the one most likely to be swayed in favor of Mr. Carter's plan," Felix whispered.

"How did you hear that?" I asked.

"When you ran to the lavatory before dinner, I wandered up to him, at first mistaking him for Mr. Carter," Felix said. "After realizing my mistake, I spoke with him for a few minutes."

"And he told you that he might be swayed by our host?" I asked.

"Yes," Felix said. "He rolled his eyes at Carter's plan, but I could see that he was only fooling himself."

I glared at him, and then straightened back up in my chair, fork in hand.

"Don't worry..." Felix murmured with a smirk, still only low enough for me to hear. "I won't leave you alone."

At least I had that assurance, as I tried to do all I could not to look at Mr. Lee. It seemed to deter him little, though, as I continued to feel his glances across the table in my direction, as I finished my dessert.

"Am I right, Mr. Crawford?"

I looked up, surprised to have a question directed to our side of the table.

"I'm sorry?" Felix asked, also caught off guard.

"The storm," asked Mr. Ward, a burly man with short, chestnut hair that did not at all match the fiery red in his thick moustache. He crossed his arms, his shoulders broad, but I wondered given the lack of definition in his limbs if he had ever worked a day in his life. "It's quite the spectacle, isn't it?"

"It certainly is," Felix said. "I've seen few like it in London."

Mr. Ward's eyes narrowed. "Though I don't expect you to understand the workings of our weather here," he said. "I always thought that everything was so much...bigger in America."

Some of the others chortled like the cronies they were.

Well done, Mr. Ward, you've showed your hand just enough for me to see that you might be the ringleader for this whole revolt against Mr. Carter.

"Oh, you can be certain that it is," Felix said. "Storms are of another world, back in New York. Isn't that right, Mr. McDonough?"

Mr. McDonough looked up, and I could feel the all too familiar tension filling the room as everyone attempted to outplay one another. "Indeed. These storms in England are tame in comparison."

I smirked, pleased that he had chosen to remain on our side. It gave me some satisfaction to be *against* Mr. Ward in any way, even if only contradicting him about the weather.

"I see," Mr. Ward said.

"It has been bad like this for weeks," Mr. Carter said at the head of the table. "Why, I could hardly get across an intersection a few days ago, the water had pooled so deep, rushing through like a dam had broken."

"The thunder has been the worst of it," said Mr. Lee. "I couldn't care less about the water. Why would I ever need to leave my car to *walk* to my place of business?"

Before anyone could respond, three servants streamed into the room from a door nearly hidden along the paneled wall near the windows, and each began to collect the empty dishes from our meal.

"Very good, thank you," Mr. Carter said as his plates were taken away. With a screech of his chair legs against the wooden floor, he stood to his feet, refastening the buttons of his jacket. "Well, now that you have all been fed and watered, I would like – "

"If you are trying to gain our favor, Carter, then likening us to horses is not a very good start," said Mr. Ward.

There was chuckling from the others.

Mr. Carter gave them a charitable smile, clapping his hands together. "I hope that you all enjoyed your dinner?"

"Decent enough," said Mr. Clayton, sitting back in his seat. "Now, what's all this about? Why are you so determined to keep us here against our wills?"

Against your wills? Is that really the best he can do?

"I have no such intention," Mr. Carter said. "I imagine you all have guessed my reason for inviting you here this evening. I had hoped to discuss my latest resolution that I proposed some weeks ago. It has been dragging on far too long, and I should like to implement – "

"Surely we could have this discussion in our offices?"

Mr. Turner asked, gesturing across the table to us. "There is no need to bore your other guests with business talk."

Mr. Carter said, "If you recall, Mr. Turner, we have had this conversation at the office, but every time I wish to sit down and speak about it, you all conveniently have meetings, or other business matters to which you must attend."

"Much like this evening, sir," Mr. Ward said, getting to his feet, buttoning the mother of pearl button on his sleeve. "I do apologize, truly I do, but I have – "

"Mr. Ward, I will ask you to give me a moment of your time," Mr. Carter interrupted. "I have been gracious, but as the head of the company, I have this authority. Even this evening, I have showed you all kindness, inviting you into my home as I have. I intend to demonstrate my level of respect for you all, by treating you not only as colleagues, but as friends. Now...sit down and give me your attention. Please."

I could see the fight in Mr. Ward's eyes. It was abundantly clear that he did not wish to listen but Mr. Carter had put him in a hard place.

A smile passed over his face, brief and forced, and he resumed his seat. "Very well," he said. "I am not an unreasonable man, as you seem determined to portray me."

I folded my arms, settling in for what was certain to be an entertaining conversation. The power struggle in the room was palpable, and the crack of thunder outside seemed all too fitting.

"Now...as I have expressed to you all on more than one occasion, this change that I am setting in place is for our betterment," Mr. Carter said. "You do not need to interject and tell me why you disagree. I am fully aware of the reasons why you do not wish to follow my lead in this matter, but I can assure you that if you look even just a few years past the ends of your noses, you will see how much better off our business will be in the long run. The money we have been setting aside for now-canceled projects has become entirely unnecessary. And at the same time, we are losing many of our most skilled workers in droves, as they seek better work conditions with our competitors. I propose to invest our extra funds into pay increases for those who work for us, building loyalty, strengthening the foundation of our own livelihoods."

Mr. Ward's expression had not softened, having instead grown more akin to stone. Mr. Turner, likewise, had taken to examining the cuff of his shirt, squinting as he inspected the weave of the fabric, as if that were much more interesting than what Mr. Carter had to say.

"I am fully aware that we have all come to benefit from the unnecessary funds raised the past few years, but they will be of even greater benefit passed on into the hands of our workers."

Mr. Clayton stifled a yawn. Mr. Lee checked his watch for the third time.

"In time, the improved health and loyalty of our employees will turn to profit, which will eventually make its way back up to us, keeping the company safe," Mr. Carter said.

Mr. Ward gave a bored sniff, looking up at the ceiling.

I thought maybe it was just as well that none of these men attempted to conceal their dislike of the plan, otherwise their intentions would be veiled...and that would make it more difficult for everyone. At least Mr. Carter knew where they stood.

"All I ask is that you consider the point," Mr. Carter continued. "I have the plan entirely written up, and have already informed some of the men under my charge that this could be coming for them, and they are elated."

"Well, Mr. Carter..." Mr. Clayton said. "Are you quite through?"

Mr. Carter seemed taken aback. "I – yes, I have said my piece," he said. "And what do you have to say for yourself?"

"I will say...we need to consider it," Mr. Clayton said. "We shall meet again in one week, and – "

"No, I would prefer that we begin putting these changes into motion over the next few days," Mr. Carter said. "And in the end, this decision is mine to make. I would much prefer that you all join me in this, that there would be no division between us – "

"We support you in a great deal," Mr. Ward said. "But in truth, we will not agree about everything."

"And it would really be an unfortunate thing for you to move forward with so little support," Mr. Turner said. "Do you really wish to make enemies?"

"On the contrary, many I have spoken with would be in favor – " Mr. Carter said.

Mr. Lee shook his head. "I think you have been had for a fool, Mr. Carter. There are many we know who dislike the idea. What if there was another major project that needed the funds? Would it not be easier to have it all stashed away for when it is needed?"

"I would agree, if the money were not being taken as

compensation," Mr. Carter said. "Do not think that I am not privy to – "

"Oh, enough," Mr. Ward said. "That is nonsense, Carter, and you know it. We keep it all above board. You know that."

Mr. Carter did not appear convinced.

Mrs. Carter, too, looked rather despairing. Her eyes, downcast to the table, seemed to shimmer in the firelight.

An enormous clap of thunder sounded outside, and the force of it shook the windows.

Mrs. Carter took the interruption as an opportunity to jump to her feet. "I must go and check on the children," she said in a rush. "Make sure they have been properly put to bed." The color in her cheeks as she hurried from the room spoke more of her frustration than any words could.

Mr. Ward got to his feet again, glaring at the window and the hammering rain. "I will tell you this, it would be unwise for us to remain out in this weather a moment longer," he said, sidestepping around his chair. "In truth, we should probably never have come in the first place, as terrible as it is. Would it not have been better for you to cancel for our wellbeing, Carter?"

Mr. Carter's expression became decidedly irritable. He glared at Mr. Ward. "I didn't want to have to resort to this...but I suppose I have no choice," he said.

The men stopped, all turning to look at their host.

"Something has recently come to my attention that would shock many of you," he said. "I have learned something about one of you...something that would ruin your reputation without fail."

A hush fell over the room, and a chill ran down my spine.

This was the reflection of the leader I had suspected lay beneath the layers of generosity.

"My purpose in inviting you all for dinner might have been cordial, but I also wished to give one of you a last chance to come clean publicly."

My heart skipped. How interesting. How very interesting.

"...And none of you has chosen to take up my offer of good will," Mr. Carter said. "So be it."

The icy quiet only deepened, and Mr. Ward turned to stare directly at Mr. Carter.

"You are no better than the rest of us," Mr. Ward spat. "Veiling your intentions with deception? What a disgrace."

Mr. Carter said nothing further as Mr. Ward turned and stomped off toward the door.

"Thank you, Carter, for a...lovely dinner," Mr. Turner said awkwardly, following after Mr. Ward.

Mr. Lee and Mr. Clayton rose as well, Mr. Lee leaving without saying a word.

Mr. Clayton turned to shake Mr. Carter's hand. "Terribly sorry about all of that, old chap. This whole affair is rather ridiculous, you know. Maybe we should set it aside for now and take a look at it again in the new year?"

Mr. Carter's eyes flashed. "I will not be delayed further," he said, his jaw clenching, and he ignored Mr. Clayton's extended hand. "As long as I am in charge, I will do what I can to see this plan through to the end. Mark my words."

Mr. Clayton shrugged his shoulders, lowering his

hand. "I understand that is your desire, but I assure you that you are too late," he said. "This is a conversation we should have been having years ago, particularly with the information you have hinted at possessing." His gaze hardened. "And what of yourself? Can you honestly tell me you did not benefit at all from those project funds we collected?"

Mr. Carter's voice became a growl. "If you are going to stand there and accuse me of dipping into those funds, then you clearly do not know me as well as you think you do, Edward."

With that, Mr. Carter strode from the room, leaving Felix and I alone with Mr. Clayton.

He did not give us any sort of consideration, however, and wandered out of the room not long after Mr. Carter.

I turned to look at Felix. "Well, that could not have gone worse."

"Forgive me for not sharing in your pessimism, sister," Felix said. "I think it was quite enlightening. Even so, I don't think we are any closer to finding the one sending the threats."

I planted my hands on my hips. "I am almost positive they are coming from that Mr. Ward," I said. "I can see it in his eyes. He despises Mr. Carter."

"Perhaps so," Felix said. "I suppose we should speak with him before the others, then?"

"It's a place to start, anyway," I said, feeling surprisingly weary. "It really could have been any of them, but I do think Mr. Ward would be the best place to begin."

Felix checked his watch, and nodded toward the door. We did not want to overstay our welcome. "Mrs. Carter will be all too happy to give us Ward's address, I'm sure,"

Felix said. "Perhaps we can go over tomorrow, but we will have to come up with a convincing reason."

"I am wondering how we are going to watch each of these men, all at the same time," I said, looking down the hall for any possible eavesdroppers. "If we turn our back on one of them to question another, how can we be sure someone we *aren't* watching won't slip in and do something drastic, like harming Mr. Carter?"

Felix said, "I think it might be best to try and remain in the shadows, keeping our eye on Carter himself."

"But that might ultimately prove to be the worst of all ideas," I said. "If any one of them – "

We had arrived in the foyer, only to find what could be considered a traffic jam near the door.

"I am sorry, sir, but I'm afraid it's impossible," said Lewis, the Carter family's butler. He held his hands outstretched toward Mr. Ward who looked about ready to barrel the door down himself.

"This is absolutely ridiculous," came the nasally voice of Mr. Turner, who pushed his glasses indignantly up his nose. "We cannot stay here."

"Stay?" Felix asked, turning to Mr. McDonough who had lingered toward the back of the group.

"The storm," Mr. McDonough explained. "It's only gotten worse."

I glanced toward the window beside the door; the rain continued to streak the glass, causing even the light out on the front steps to become bleary. "It doesn't appear any worse than it was some hours ago," I said.

"We have been waiting for our cars to be brought around," said Mr. Clayton, just ahead of Mr. McDonough. "But they aren't coming."

"Because of the rain?" Felix asked.

The door opened, and Mr. Carter stepped inside, nearly sodden to the core, wiping rain from his eyes. "My apologies, but there is no way anyone is going to be able to leave," he said as Lewis helped him shrug off his soaked coat. The rain continued to pelt the front steps behind him, a wall of water that constantly shimmered and changed.

"What do you mean?" Mr. Lee snapped. "I have appointments that I must keep."

"I'm sorry," Mr. Carter said, running his fingers through his dripping hair to smooth it flat against his head. "The roads have entirely flooded. Some of the cars won't even start."

Mr. Ward pushed Mr. Carter aside and strode out through the open door and into the stormy night. A roll of thunder made the very walls shake, no longer dampened by the closed door.

"It doesn't seem as if the rains have any intention of stopping, either," Mr. Carter said. "It is for your own safety that you remain here."

"Are you saying we have no choice but to stay?" Mr. Turner asked.

Mr. Carter nodded. "I'm afraid so, unless you wish to brave the elements and take your life into your hands."

Mr. Turner's sour expression hardened as he turned to stare out through the doorway. His jaw muscles worked as if chewing on words that he was considering speaking.

"You are all going to have to wait it out here," Mr. Carter said. "As soon as the rains slow, and some of the water drains from the streets, it will be safer to go. Of

course, each of you is the judge of when you wish to leave
– "

Mr. Ward shouldered Mr. Carter as he passed, a nasty grimace set firmly on his broad face. "There's no way we can leave," he barked. "Nearly killed myself walking up those stairs, and was up to my knees in water out there." He gestured down to his legs, which contrary to his dramatic statement, only showed damp around the hems of his trousers.

"That's it, then?" Mr. Clayton asked. "We're stranded here?"

"Yes, you're stranded here..." Mr. Carter said. "Until the storm passes."

"It's been raining for the past three days," Mr. Turner spat.

"I realize that," Mr. Carter said. He sighed heavily, glancing over at Lewis. "Shall we fetch some tea and what is left of the trifle, then?"

Mr. Turner groaned, and Mr. Clayton shook his head.

I looked up at Felix, my eyebrows rising.

What an unfortunate turn of events to be trapped in a house full of people who hate one another...

6

There were lines drawn as soon as Mr. Carter's declaration was made. These men had no intention of remaining in his presence, and that being the case, practically barricaded themselves in the dining room. It was rather unceremonious, with much grunting and groaning, and obvious glaring stares and snide remarks as they left. While they had no intention of spending any more time with Mr. Carter, they were likely not going to be above enjoying the luxuries of his hospitality.

Mr. McDonough, however, deemed it unwise to mingle with them, and as such, decided to retire back to the drawing room where we had begun the evening. Felix and I assured him that we would accompany him soon, but I had something else I needed to do first.

"We should have a word with our driver," I said. "He ought to be informed of our decision to stay."

As if on cue, the front door opened, and all of the drivers came hurrying inside, one right after the other.

No one could blame them for using the front door, under the circumstances, since the way to the servant's entrance was probably flooded. As they gathered around the foyer, a small lake formed in the midst of their soaked boots.

Our own chauffeur came in last, closely followed by Lewis. The door was closed, the rain and winds outside dying down, muffled by the walls and windows.

"Ronald, are you quite all right?" I asked.

His boots and clothing made squishing sounds as he moved. "Oh, I'm fine, Miss Crawford," he said, removing his hat which dripped like the edge of a roof, and giving it a look over. "The car, though, I'm not so sure about. Mr. Sansbury may not be too pleased if we can't get it up and running once it dries out a bit." He turned to look over his shoulder. "...Which may not be for a long time, at this rate."

Felix said, "You must be soaked to the bone."

Ronald held up his arm, and water dripped from the ends of his sleeve. "A little, sir," he said. "Though there comes a point where one cannot be any wetter."

"You'll catch your death like this," I said, frowning at him.

He shrugged. "I'll be all right. Just need to stand in front of a fire for a bit."

"What happened out there?" Felix asked. "Has it really gotten that much worse?"

"You would think it impossible, but it did," Ronald said. "I became worried when the water rose enough to slosh up onto the sidewalks like a tide coming in."

My eyes widened. "It's really that deep?"

"It is. It started to pool in the street, and then it became more akin to a river," he said. He sighed. "There is likely no way we will be leaving any time soon. Perhaps not until morning."

My heart sank. "Morning? Do you really think so?"

"We can hope for the best, Miss," Ronald said. "But I cannot see the rains ending, and even if they do slow, it will take time for all of that water to run off."

I looked at Felix, who shrugged, sliding his hands into his pockets.

We were stranded, just as much as the other guests were...and there was nothing we could do about it.

Footsteps echoed in the hall behind me, and I turned to see Mrs. Carter enter the foyer. She had changed during her time upstairs, having shifted from her gauzy dress to something a little plainer and more comfortable. "Oh, my heavens..." she said, hurrying into the room. "Look at you all. You must be positively freezing."

Mr. Carter came in after her, looking rather cross. He still wore his own rain-drenched clothes. I imagined he must not have had a chance to change as he attempted to handle the mess that was quickly unfolding around him. "Well, at least you are all out of the storm," he said.

"Darling, we cannot let them stay like this," Mrs. Carter said, turning to her husband.

"Indeed," Mr. Carter said, eyeing the new swimming pool that had taken the place of his foyer floor.

"Lewis, we must get them cleaned up," she said. "I am certain there are extra clothes down in storage some-where, aren't there? These men can't stay like this all night."

"You're right, of course," Mr. Carter said. "Lewis, would you mind escorting them down to the kitchens and finding them someplace to dry out?"

"Certainly, sir," Lewis said, sidestepping around a slightly befuddled looking driver who seemed far too old to be chauffeuring. "This way, please."

Ronald gave us a quick smile before trailing after the others.

"And make sure that you get this mess in the foyer cleaned up as well, Lewis," Mr. Carter called after them, then snapped his fingers. "Oh, blast. I needed to speak with him about something else. Excuse me, I shan't be long."

"I hope not, dear," Mrs. Carter said as he hurried down the hall after Lewis. "I won't quite know how to take care of these guests..."

They had all gone their way, and we were left alone with Mrs. Carter.

She stared down the hall until the very last sight of Mr. Carter's coat tails had vanished before she hurried over to us. "You must accept my deepest apologies..." she said in a hurried tone. "I cannot believe that this night is turning out the way it is. I do not think I could have imagined a worse experience."

"It's all right, Mrs. Carter," Felix said. "You need not be so hard on yourself. How are the children?"

"Oh, they're perfectly all right," she said. "Two of them were long asleep when I checked on them, and the others only needed some encouragement from myself and their nanny before they settled in as well. That made me feel better, but I still cannot quiet my heart about what has gone on these past few hours. I am simply appalled at my husband's associates and their attitudes. How could they so easily dismiss what he had to say?"

"I'm afraid it is clear not one of them has any respect for him," I said.

"If I had known the dinner was going to go so poorly, I would have reconsidered inviting the both of you here this evening," she said. "Now my whole idea feels foolish, as it seems your presence here has caused somewhat of a stir and likely aroused their suspicions as to the reason for it."

"I am not terribly surprised," I said, folding my arms. "I had not realized the dinner was so exclusive."

"Yes, I suppose in my panic, I thought it perfectly reasonable to ask you here so that you might take a good look at them..." She turned a hopeful gaze upon me. "You haven't formed any theories yet about which of them might be the person who has been threatening us, have you?"

"Not yet, Mrs. Carter, I'm sorry," I said. "Not to distress you, but it honestly could have been any one of them, given their mutual dislike of your husband and his plans."

She gave a great sigh, and shook her head. "It hasn't always been this way, you know. I used to rather like these men, some ten years ago or so. You see, my husband has known these gentlemen for...well, for nearly a quarter of a century. It has only been in recent years that everything has changed."

"It seems that many of them are in complete agreement with one another, at least in regards to their stance against your husband's plans," Felix said. "I must admit, I am impressed at his decision to stand his ground."

"As am I," she said, though worry tugged at her brow. "His stubborn courage is one of the many reasons I married him. However, in this situation, it seems almost as if it would be wiser for me to try and talk him out of his plans, for the safety of our family."

"I would not go so far as to say that, Mrs. Carter," I said. "You have hired us to find the person behind all these attacks, and we intend to do just that. We may not have been able to pinpoint him yet, but you need not worry that we will find him, because we will. I can promise you."

Her face split into a relieved smile. "Thank you," she said. "I don't know why I allowed myself to become so frazzled this evening. It isn't as if I didn't already know tonight would be difficult."

"Consider this, though," I said. "There could not be a better place for us this evening, given our investigating. I doubt we will have the chance to speak with these men all together in the same room again, and we intend to take full advantage of the opportunity. Right, Felix?"

"Indeed we do," Felix said. "We now have the time to speak with them, time that we would have had to carve out at a later date. This means the investigation could be over that much sooner."

"All of these men might despise your husband, Mrs. Carter, but after speaking with each of them for even a short time, someone who hates him enough to send threatening messages should be easy enough to sniff out," I said. *And I already have an inkling of who it might be.*

Mrs. Carter wrapped her arms tightly around herself, and cast a mournful look down the hall at her husband. "To be honest, I do not care at all what methods you choose to take in order to find the culprit," she said in a low voice. "My husband's life is far too precious, and I will not stand in your way if there are less than savory methods you must employ to navigate this situation. All I ask is that you allow me to remain naïve of whatever you must resort to."

I smirked at her. "While I appreciate your willingness to trust us, I assure you there will be nothing terribly devious going on under your roof."

"Yes, we keep our work above board," Felix said. "You need not worry about us crossing the law or any such."

"Speaking of the law," I said, using his comment as a jumping off point. "Depending on how things go this evening, you may need to consider the possibility of involving the police, given the seriousness of your concerns – "

A strike of lightning lit up the whole foyer in brilliant, white light, quickly followed by a crack of thunder as loud as a firearm going off. The noise echoed through the night…

Then my vision went dark.

7

"Is everyone all right?"

Felix's voice pierced the velvety darkness pressing in all around me. I reached out and the tips of my fingers brushed against the wool of his jacket. I fumbled a bit, trying to find his hand, as blind as a bat in the daylight.

"Yes," I said, with a shakiness in my voice that I hardly recognized. It was not like me to become so easily rattled.

"I'm fine," Mrs. Carter said from somewhere to my right. "The storm must have taken out the power."

I blinked furiously, trying to see something, *anything*.

Felix tugged on my hand, and I obliged, but slowly. Suddenly I feared careening down a flight of stairs, or tripping over a loose floorboard, perhaps even stubbing my toe on some large statue –

"Let's stand here near the wall," Felix said. "This way we won't be in anyone's way."

"Good thinking," I said.

"It's even dark out through the window," Mrs. Carter

said. "At least, I think it is. I can scarcely tell which way is up."

I reached out with my free hand, and my fingers bumped into Mrs. Carter's shoulder. "Oh, my apologies," I said. I reached out again, this time grazing the wall of the foyer.

I let out a small exhale of relief. At least I could orient myself with the wall.

"That means the whole neighborhood has gone dark," Felix said. "If not the whole city."

"The whole city?" I asked.

"If that's the case, then there will be no telling when the lights are going to come back on..." Mrs. Carter said in a wavering tone.

I pinched my eyes shut tight, and when I opened them, I realized I could now just make out shapes and outlines in the darkness.

Across the room, I could see the outline of the window, and the dark streaks of rain like wet ink running trails down the glass. Everything seemed much louder; the rain pounded harder, the thunder in the distance sounded deeper, and the sounds of shuffling movement around the house made me wonder if a hoard of mice had taken up residence underneath the floorboards.

"This is not good..." Mrs. Carter said. "The night has only just begun. It is going to be hours before there is any sort of light in the sky, and that's if the storm lets up at all to let any light through."

It certainly seemed disquieting to think, but really, the storm was of little threat to us indoors.

A brilliant, yellow light appeared out of the corner of my eye. "Look!" I exclaimed, turning to point.

A golden orb, dim at first, grew in size and brightness, until I realized that it was light bouncing off the wooden panels of the wall, a reflection of the real source that came around the corner.

It was Lewis, carrying a glowing candelabra, following closely behind Mr. Carter.

"Darling, is everyone all right?" Mr. Carter asked, hurrying over to his wife.

"Oh, yes," Felix said. "We were just speaking with your wife when the lights went out."

"Howard, the children must be frightened," Mrs. Carter said. "You know how they hate this sort of thing, and Nanny is hardly reassuring. I must go and check on them myself."

"Of course," Mr. Carter said. He turned to a narrow table just inside the front door, and after fumbling around in the drawer for a moment, produced a slender candle. He deposited it into a lantern that sat decoratively on top of the table, before plucking one of the candles from the butler's candelabra, and lighting the wick of the new candle. He closed the glass door of the lantern, and handed it to his wife. "There. Find one of the maids to help you light more candles upstairs."

Mrs. Carter nodded, taking the lantern in a shaky hand. She cast me a furtive glance before turning to hurry up the stairs.

"The staff are rounding up all the candles they can," he called after her. "I will go and inform the rest of the guests."

"I won't be long," she said.

Mr. Carter gave a great sigh, and instead of turning around as I had expected him to, he approached Felix and me. "My deepest apologies," he said. "This evening has not gone quite the way that I had planned."

"It's no trouble at all, Mr. Carter," Felix said. "How could you know the storm would grow this severe?"

"Well, it isn't as if I blame myself, really," Mr. Carter said. "But that does not prevent my wishing this evening's gathering had taken place at a different time. Who knows, though? Perhaps there would have been some other terrible event to take place. One can never avoid disaster entirely."

"No, I suppose we cannot," I said.

"In a way, I am grateful that you are here," Mr. Carter added, running his hands through his still damp hair, trying to dry it. "Your presence is a welcome distraction for my wife. She seems to have taken to you both, and as she distresses easily in times of tension, I am thankful she has someone she *likes* to speak with on hand."

"Oh, I don't know if that is entirely necessary," Felix said. "She was just telling us how you and your associates have all known one another for a long, long time."

"Yes, well...a lot can change in that amount of time." Mr. Carter said, and he took a moment to glance down the hall as Lewis set the candelabra on a table beside the door. "I suppose I should have everyone convene in the drawing room. It might be easier to keep one room lit rather than the entire house."

"A good suggestion," Felix said.

"Here, don't go without light," Mr. Carter said. He reached for another candle that Lewis had lit, and handed it to Felix. He looked around and snatched up a linen table runner, and handed that to him as well. "For the wax drips."

"On your fine linen, sir?" Felix asked.

Mr. Carter shrugged. "It's either that or your hand, and I would rather pick the wax out than have to send my housekeeper down to fetch the gauze and the salve for your burns. Besides, I am sure Mrs. Carter would never turn down an opportunity to buy new linens for our home. Do you remember where the drawing room is?"

"Yes," I said. "Down the next hall, up the small set of stairs, and to the left."

"Exactly," he said. "I shall join you as soon as I round up the gentlemen in the dining room. I hope the candles from the table have not burned down all the way."

Felix offered his arm to me, and together we turned and started down the hall.

"Well, this is an adventure, isn't it?" I asked in a low voice as we made our way, still slowly, down the hall. Despite the dim light, we were unfamiliar with the house, and it would not be impossible to trip or injure ourselves in some way in the dark. "The evening has just gone from bad to worse."

"I will say that the whole affair is unsettling," Felix said. "I came into this evening thinking we would just have to be on our guard about this dinner, and then we had no choice but to stay and wait out the storm. Now there are no lights..."

"Mr. Carter is working to get more candles together. It won't be dark like this for long," I said.

"I am not worried about that. But the tension that was so thick at dinner...I don't imagine it will have gone away."

"Well, perhaps Mr. Carter can sit these men down and talk to them," I said. "They have no choice but to stay here, and likely nothing better to do than listen. Maybe they can come to some kind of resolution, and we will be able to drop the case all together."

Felix looked down at me, and pursed his lips in consideration. "That's an interesting point," he said. "Let's hope that's how the evening goes. Otherwise, maybe we can push the conversation in that direction."

"Of course," I said. "We would be able to make sure they are all in the same room, make sure they don't leave...maybe even stand in the doorway if they try to – "

We rounded the corner, and dim light stretched across the hall, coming through the open doorway to the drawing room.

We found Mr. McDonough standing with one of the servants at the round card table, using a lit candle to light a four-pronged candelabra, almost a dozen taper candles lying beside it, waiting to be used. He looked up as we entered.

"Oh, I wondered where you had gotten off to," he said, swiftly turning his attention back to the candelabra.

"You found yourself some light, I see," I said, making my way to him. Somehow, it felt better to have the company of people nearby. It made the darkness feel a bit less oppressive.

"Yes, thankfully Walter here was in tending to the fireplace when I arrived, and knew right where to find candles when the lights went out, as well as an oil lamp." He gestured to the low table sitting between the two sofas, where the comfortable glow of a lamp flickered lazily.

"Glad to hear it," Felix said.

"What's happening out there?" Mr. McDonough

asked as the servant called Walter took the candle from him, and continued to light the candelabra for him. "Is everyone all right?"

"Yes, as far as we could see," I said. "Mr. Carter has gone to fetch – "

Voices down the hall filled in the rest of my broken statement, and I pointed with a shrug.

The other four members of the guild streamed into the room, closely followed by Mr. Carter and the butler.

"I understand, but I will have Lewis bring whatever you need," Mr. Carter said, speaking to Mr. Turner, who was looking over his shoulder, glaring at him. "I realize this is not anyone's ideal for this evening, but we might as well make the best of it."

Mr. Ward crossed his arms. "What do you propose we do now, then?" he asked.

Mr. Carter looked about. "Well...Of course I have cards, but if anyone would rather play another game, I might be able to oblige. Apart from that, there is always time for tea and conversation..."

Yes, conversation. That would be the best use of our time.

"You cannot tell me you must be entertained at all hours of the day," Mr. McDonough said, carrying the oil lamp to a darker corner on the far side of the room, away from the fire. It thinned the shadows along the edges of the parlor, but darkened the middle of the space. "You are men of business. Surely you realize patience is part of the process?"

"That isn't the point," Mr. Ward said. "This sort of idleness is doing nothing to make us more profit, is it?"

Mr. McDonough shrugged. "Perhaps not you. I left

my businesses in good hands back in the States. There is no such thing as idle time in my world."

Mr. Ward's glare deepened.

"What of some music?" Felix asked, gesturing to the piano tucked in the corner near the window. "Perhaps a few songs would lift our spirits?"

"This is hardly the time for such frivolities," Mr. Turner said, the lenses of his glasses flashing in the firelight. "This evening was meant to be a business meeting, not a gathering for pleasantries."

"Well, why couldn't it be just that?" I asked, shrugging. "Wouldn't it make the time pass more swiftly?"

Mr. Turner seemed to have no answer for that.

Good. This means they will have no choice but to sit and talk. This can only work in Mr. Carter's favor.

"Why don't we get a game of cards going, then?" Felix asked. "I would certainly be happy to set one up."

There were murmurs of noncommittal agreement all around.

Felix looked at me, and I shrugged. What else were we going to do?

Mr. Carter looked around at all of us before clapping his hands together. "Excellent. I will leave you to begin a game. I shall want to be dealt a hand next round, but for the time being, I will go see to more candles, perhaps some fresh pots of tea, and then see if my wife or children are in need of anything. Come along, Lewis. Let's take care of this."

I followed him over to the door with my eyes, sighing. It seemed there was nothing else we could do apart from waiting. I wandered to the card table which Felix had walked to, but no one else seemed entirely ready to move.

I turned to look at them all, still gathered around near the door.

"What is your plan?" I asked Felix in a low voice. "Hoping to relieve these men of a little extra money?"

Felix smirked at me as he pulled a deck from one of the handsomely painted sleeves and began to shuffle. "Perhaps..." he said. "I imagine they have not played a real game of cards in some time. It might be fun."

"Don't upset them too much," I said. "Mr. Carter will want to – "

"I don't believe that we have been properly introduced..." came a voice far too close to my elbow.

I turned to see Mr. Lee standing beside me, staring at me in the same rude manner he had over the dinner table earlier. He was crowding so near I could feel his hot breath against my shoulder.

I felt a flash of annoyance that even Felix must have sensed, for he spoke up quickly before I could snap at the man to take a step back.

"Ah, Mr. Lee..." Felix said over the top of my head. "No, I suppose you have not been introduced. This is my sister, Miss Crawford."

"How very pleased I am to make your acquaintance. Did I hear your brother say your name was...Lillian?" Mr. Lee asked.

"It is," I admitted, noting the unappealing way sweat beaded on his upper lip.

His grin spread, and he folded his hands in front of himself. "What a lovely name, befitting such a *lovely* young woman."

"You are not the first to think so," Felix interjected casually on my behalf. He must have sensed my annoyance and been anxious to head off an unpleasant scene. "She is practically engaged, but the lucky gentleman could not be here tonight, as he is a very busy man. He has been performing every night for the past two weeks in some of London's most prominent theaters."

Mr. Lee's eyes narrowed. "And who is this man?"

"Mr. Eugene Osbourn," I said.

Mr. Lee smirked, and his eyes flashed. "I've never heard of him."

I felt strangely indignant. Never heard of him? I had yet to come across a person who had never heard Eugene's name.

"The formerly blind concert pianist," Felix said. "He is world famous. How unfortunate you have not had the opportunity to hear him. But I suppose he does have quite *exclusive* performances, and one must have the right connections."

Mr. Lee's expression hardened like hot metal hitting frigid water. "I have little time for such frivolities as concerts and entertainments," he snapped.

"How unfortunate for you..." I began, eyes narrowing.

My brother must have decided it was time to escape the conversation. "One moment, Mr. McDonough," Felix said over his shoulder, holding his hand to his ear. "Mr. Lee, I am terribly sorry, but you will have to excuse us. This conversation has been...most interesting. Perhaps you will join us for a game of cards shortly?"

"Certainly," Mr. Lee said with a sneer. "I shall be happy to. I used to play cards a great deal, you see. Became rather good."

Felix's eyes flashed, and a corner of his mouth

twitched upward. "I implore you, sir, to show me your skill soon."

With that, Felix pressed a hand against the small of my back and steered me away from the card table.

"Quick thinking, finding a way out of that conversation," I congratulated him, as we stopped beside Mr. McDonough. "It might have ended poorly for everyone within earshot."

Mr. McDonough glanced up, snapping the book closed. "Speaking with Mr. Lee, I see?" he asked. "I assume you used my name as a distraction?"

"Thank you for being willing to be used as one," Felix said.

Mr. McDonough nodded, sliding the book into its designated space up on the shelf. "Happy to do so. What is it that you – "

"My apologies for the interruption, but I thought we were to be playing cards," said an unfamiliar voice behind us.

I turned, and Mr. Ward stood there behind us, his hair...or lack thereof...haloed by the flickering amber light of the fire.

"Ah, Mr. Ward," Mr. McDonough said, a look of veiled irritation flitting across his face.

"We just need a quick word with Mr. McDonough," Felix told Mr. Ward. "Then I will be happy to deal a hand or two."

"Well, I have a question to ask first," Mr. Ward said, a blaze in his eyes. "Specifically, I would very much like to know why the pair of you Crawfords happen to be here this evening?"

I blinked at him. That was a rather strange question,

wasn't it? For it to be so out of the blue, had we done something to tip him off? "We were invited by Mrs. Carter," I said, quite plainly. It was the truth, so it was much easier to put weight behind the words, along with the glare I equipped.

Mr. Ward shook his head, a mirthless smile spreading over his face. Clearly, he was not the sort with a sense of humor. "I have no idea who you are. I have never *heard* of you. So why is it that you are here, on this night of all nights, when we are speaking about private business matters?"

I gestured behind me at Mr. McDonough. "Pardon me, Mr. Ward, but is Mr. McDonough a part of this business of yours?"

Mr. Ward spared Mr. McDonough a brief glance, his expression growing fiercer. "No, but I am well aware of who Mr. McDonough is, and his relationship to Mr. Carter. You, however, I do not know. How can I be certain you were not sent here by a rival company trying to steal information? Or working with the authorities, attempting to pin something on us that we have not done?"

My eyes narrowed. "Why do you assume there is some dark purpose to our presence, Mr. Ward? Surely Mrs. Carter has the right to invite whomever she wishes to a dinner party in her home?"

"I can assure you, Mr. Ward, you have nothing to worry about with this pair," Mr. McDonough said. "I am well acquainted with their father back in New York."

Mr. Ward's gaze sharpened. "And just who is their father?"

"Mr. Crawford of *Crawford and Yale*," Mr. McDonough said.

I noticed the slightest change in Mr. Ward's expression, shifting from anger to worry.

Felix adjusted his collar beside me. "I am the heir to my father's financial empire," he said. "I have come to England so that I might receive special training from a relative, who is also in finance. Perhaps you know him; Mr. Richard Sansbury?"

Mr. Ward swallowed, and he looked away, even more cross than he had been before.

"And my sister here is soon to be engaged to Mr. Eugene Osbourn, the famous concert pianist," Felix added. "As well as being a partial heiress to my father's company."

Mr. Ward seemed to be chewing his tongue to pieces inside his mouth, breathing through his nose. His gaze snapped to Mr. McDonough. "Is this true?"

"Every word of it," Mr. McDonough said, though he looked at me with a hint of surprise.

I remembered that my relationship with Eugene was not yet widely known, and I shifted uncomfortably. I hoped it wouldn't get back to him that I had been sharing around town the claim that we were all but engaged. But he would surely understand the need for my exaggeration under the circumstances, wouldn't he?

Mr. Ward stared back and forth between Felix and me. "This still does not explain *why* you are here this evening," he said.

It amazed me just how easy it had become to lie in these circumstances. I was me, and yet at the same time, was playing the part of a different persona entirely. I stared at him, keeping my expression placid. "From what I know, there were two other couples who were meant to be here this evening, on Mrs. Carter's invitation, but one had to cancel due to an illness, and the other for some conflicting, prior engagement."

"Which is a shame, really," Felix said. "I had hoped I would have the chance to speak with Mr. Thomas. I have only met him the once, and it was some years ago."

Thank you, Felix, for following my lead on this.

"*I* was under the impression this gathering was intended to be a pleasant evening's entertainment among friends of the Carters," I said, glancing up at Mr. McDonough. "And as we *are* all friends or associates of Mr. Carter, I simply cannot understand the lack of support for his business plans. Can you, Mr. McDonough?"

Mr. McDonough seemed somewhat caught off guard by the change in topic. He cleared his throat. "It certainly is a surprise that he seems to have met such opposition, after guiding the company so ably for so long. Surely everyone trusts him?"

"It's unfathomable, really," Felix added, for good measure.

Mr. Ward's face soured further. "Thank you for sharing your opinions so freely," he said, his tone anything but sincere. "If you will excuse me, I should like to go and check on the car situation, see if we are any closer to being able to leave. I have an important meeting in the morning that I absolutely cannot miss."

With that, he turned around and stalked toward the darkened doorway, slipping out into the blackness.

"Well...I think we know full well where these men really stand," I murmured, when he was gone. "We all witnessed their great dislike of Mr. Carter, and any changes he wishes to make. The only question is how far are they prepared to go to thwart him?"

Thunder rolled overhead, and I sighed, staring at the window. No lights shone in the city, only our own reflections. The room went quiet, as if we all waited for something.

It feels as if the storm is right over the top of us.

Then a scream echoed through the blackness of the manor...

8

My stomach dropped to the floor, and my head whipped around.

I found Felix staring at me, mirroring my own expression of dread.

It couldn't be.

But how many reasons were there for someone to scream like that? I *knew* the sound of that scream, the pain and terror behind it. It might have come from a different mouth every time, but it was the same...always the same.

Without another word, without a single moment to lose, Felix and I turned as one and dashed toward the door. He reached the doorway before me, with his long legs, but quickly turned away before he breached the barrier of shadows.

I looked wildly around as people moved and called out behind me, until my eyes fell upon a narrow candlestick. I snatched it off the nearby table and hurried to Felix's side, as he moved forward.

A shallow pool of light spread out from my candle, barely reaching the opposite wall of the corridor.

I tried to swallow, but my throat had gone as dry as stone.

My hand trembled as I held the candle aloft, trying to see something, anything.

Felix reached out and grabbed the back of my hand, steadying me.

"Come on, let's stay together..." he said, taking the candle from me, as we started down the hall.

We didn't have to traverse long before a silhouette appeared out of the darkness.

"Mrs. Carter," Felix said, hurrying forward, with me close behind him.

As we came up beside her...we finally saw what it was that had caused the terrible scream.

A still body lay sprawled across the middle of the corridor. In the dim, wavering light of our candle, all I could make out were a leg and an arm, stretched out across the antique runner.

The tense knots twisted around my insides all seemed to drop at once...only to be replaced with a vast, sickening hollowness.

An hour might have passed, or perhaps it was only the length of a few heartbeats. It didn't matter, as it didn't change the scene before me.

Mrs. Carter trembled and sobbed into her hands beside me, and it drew me out of my own shock. Felix started toward her, and as he did, I smoothly took the candle back from him, knowing we had best play to our strengths. He was better at getting information out of people who were distraught, I was better at examining a scene of violence.

I steeled myself, and approached the body.

As I drew nearer, light spilled over the figure, revealing more of it with each step. First, the trousers of a fine suit. Next, a torso clothed in a linen shirt, exposed by the hem of a suit coat folded back on itself, revealing the purple silk lining inside. Then, there were the mother of pearl cufflinks along the sleeve...

I found the man's head last, and to my horror...I saw the face of Mr. Lee, his eyes wide, staring unseeing at some distant place.

It was clear he was gone, with no rise and fall of his back, no light in his eyes, no movement of any kind. It did not take a great deal of detective work to see precisely how it was that he met his end. The trickle of blood from his temple down along his jawline could clearly be traced to a nasty wound at the back of his head, the blood glistening as black as ink in the dimness of the hall.

My heartbeat hammered in my ears, the only sound I heard.

How long had it been since we had spoken to him? It couldn't have been more than a quarter of an hour? Perhaps not even that long since he had evidently drifted out of the drawing room?

I took a hesitant step back, Mrs. Carter's muffled sobs echoing off the polished wood paneling of the hall.

How could anyone have done this so quickly? And how and why had they done it?

I drew in a few deep breaths through my mouth, hoping to bypass the metallic stench of the blood. I knew

I had to take a closer look before anyone else came to investigate the scream, so I knelt closer to the corpse.

I overcame my distaste long enough to gingerly take his wrist in my free hand and feel for a pulse, just to be sure he was past all help. I was unsurprised to find none, and set his hand down again. I was thankful that, even with the light in my other hand, the wound on the dead man's head was difficult to see too clearly. Even so, what was clear was that he had been struck with something heavy.

I straightened and held the candle out, willing my eyes to see further into the darkness. When they would not, I took a quick lap around Mr. Lee's body, careful not to disturb or move him in any way. I checked the floor for footprints near the pool of blood that had seeped into the rug, but saw none. I looked for anything large, anything that could have been used to bludgeon him...and found nothing. There were some small trinkets lining the hall in low shelves or resting on narrow tables, but nothing sizable enough to kill a man. I noticed a rather lovely vase, but knew at once it could not be the weapon, as it would have shattered upon impact, not to mention the noise it would have made.

What could it have been, then?

It was clever timing, all things considered. Someone could have sneaked up on him easily in the dark, and a strike to the head with something heavy would likely have killed him instantly.

I gave the corpse one more look over to see if I had missed anything, but it really was quite straightforward. He had been struck down, without attracting the notice of anyone else in the manor.

At least...to my current knowledge.

The sound of rapidly approaching footsteps announced that the others who had been in the drawing room or scattered nearby now hurried down the hall. They were closely followed by Lewis, who carried his trusty candelabra. In the commotion, I turned to look. All the guests seemed accounted for.

I stepped aside, moving away from Mr. Lee's body and taking my place beside Mrs. Carter and Felix.

Mr. Carter appeared at the head of the approaching pack. "What on earth was that scream?"

Mrs. Carter let out a wail, and ran down the hall to her husband, throwing herself into his arms.

Mr. Carter stopped in his tracks, but it only took him a moment to find the source of his wife's consternation... and for all the color I could see in the dimness to drain from his face.

I had witnessed this scene more than once. The shock and horror written on the faces of each observer; the jaws falling open, eyes widening. Mr. Clayton turned and wretched into a nearby corner, out of our sight. Mr. Turner reached out and grabbed hold of the wall. Mr. Ward's hands balled into fists at his side.

"What has happened here?" Mr. Ward demanded, his voice wobbling with desperation or shock.

"It seems that Mr. Lee has been fatally attacked," I said, surprising myself with the calmness of my words. "I have checked for a pulse, but I fear he is beyond our help."

It took mere seconds for everyone to digest my words, and then the group erupted into tumult.

Mr. Ward thrust out an accusatory hand, his finger

extended like the point of a blade toward Mr. Carter. "Carter, what have you done?"

"I have done nothing," Mr. Carter protested, stepping between his wife and Mr. Ward.

"This happened in *your house,* Carter!" Mr. Ward thundered, his voice rivaling the storm still rolling past above our heads.

"As if I am to control the actions of every person beneath my roof?" Mr. Carter asked.

"It is your responsibility!" Mr. Ward insisted.

"Ward, calm yourself," Mr. Clayton said, trying to raise his voice over Mr. Ward's. "We mustn't fall to accusing one another."

Mr. McDonough stepped further into the light as well, and it surprised me; I hadn't heard him approach with the others. He glanced for a moment toward the body, and then his gaze shifted to me.

I could see in his eyes that he was beginning to put some of the missing pieces together. My brother and I had been the ones to investigate the murder on the ship, and here was yet another death that happened right under our noses. I could see the question there in his gaze, and knew he would bring it to me as soon as he could. He was beginning to wonder like everyone else about our true purpose in being there.

"Let's all take a breath," he said in his deep, smooth voice. "The worst thing we could do right now is – "

"Who found him?" Mr. Ward interrupted, turning around to look at each of us in turn, his eyes flashing. "Who screamed out here in the hall?"

"Mrs. Carter," Felix said, stepping between myself and Mr. Ward.

I glanced sidelong at Mrs. Carter. I couldn't quite make out her expression in the dark, her face hidden by her husband's shadow, but she hung her head, one hand clutching the back of his jacket with a tight fist.

"Well, then," Mr. Ward said, his eyes flashing. "Perhaps *she* is the one who – "

"Don't you *dare* accuse my wife!" Mr. Carter snapped, taking a step toward Mr. Ward.

"Can you prove it wasn't her?" Mr. Ward cried, matching his motion. "How could you know for certain if you weren't present when it happened?"

"She didn't do it," I said.

I didn't have to shout like the others, but still I was heard. Each pair of eyes turned to look at me.

I stiffened, holding my head higher. "Mrs. Carter isn't the one who killed him, she is simply the one who found him."

"How do you know?" Mr. Turner asked, still not having let go of the wall; I wondered if the room was spinning for him. "How can you be so certain?"

"Look at her," I said. "The poor woman is utterly terrified. She could barely speak when we came out here. Besides, she wouldn't have been strong enough to strike a man in the back of the head and kill him instantly."

"Strike him in the – how do you know so much?" Mr. Ward demanded.

I gestured to Mr. Lee's body, lying just a short distance away. "It's obvious, given the wound at the back of his head."

Mr. Ward's brow furrowed, but he was slow to take a look in Mr. Lee's direction...and when he did, his eyes did not linger long. "You seem quite knowledgeable about how he died already..." he growled. "How do we know you did not do this?"

"Because I was in the drawing room with others when he was found," I pointed out. "I did not leave that room after entering it when the lights went out. My brother and I had spoken to Mr. Lee just moments before you came to speak with us. You, and Mr. McDonough."

Though it seems people filtered in and out of that room, without my taking much notice...

I looked over again at Mr. McDonough, who had largely remained silent. "She's right," he said. "She or her brother couldn't have done this, as they were with me."

"Then who *did*?" Mr. Ward barked.

"That is what we are going to find out," Mr. Carter said, staring around, his jaw set. "*I* am going to find out. A man has died in my home, a man whom I once respected, and not only died...but has quite obviously been killed." He steeled himself, as if puffing up. "I know that the guilty party is in this house, among us. I just need to discover who it is."

Apart from the hammering rain and the rumbling thunder, the long stretch of hall went eerily silent. The severe weight of the moment, of the realization that what he said was most certainly true...seemed to hang over us as thick and dark as the shadows themselves.

"Everyone return to the drawing room," Mr. Carter said. "Nobody leave. I am going to send for the police, and they will deal with this matter as they see fit."

"But we have done nothing wrong," Mr. Clayton protested.

"That's right," Mr. Ward agreed with him. "You cannot

stand there, Carter, and tell us what we can and cannot –
"

Mr. Carter took two long strides to the wall, almost entirely out of the light, snatched something off the wall, and whirled around with a glinting blade in his hand.

Mrs. Carter shrieked, and everyone else took a step backward, away from him.

Upon closer inspection, it looked like an antiquated military blade, given the shape of the hilt and the faded, indecipherable inscription on the blade itself. Mr. Carter held it in a steady hand, demonstrating what must be a great familiarity and knowledge of swordsmanship. He held it as if it was simply an extension of his right arm, and he pointed the tip squarely at Mr. Ward's chest.

"You will do as I say," Mr. Carter said in a low tone, his eyes flashing. "You will not fool me into believing that one of you is not responsible, for I know otherwise. It was not myself, nor my wife, nor any member of my staff who would have committed such a – such a heinous crime. It could only be one of you despicable creatures, and you will not convince me otherwise. Now...I am not going to repeat myself. All of you, get to the drawing room, and stay there. The storm has made it impossible to telephone, but I will send a servant to fetch the police...and you can expect that I will be sharing fully with them what I know of you."

He waved the end of his sword down the hall, ushering everyone onward.

Mr. Ward's eyes narrowed. "Very well, Carter. But rest assured that I will not hide what I know from the authorities, either. If I am going down, then I am going to take you with me."

With that, he turned and started off back down the corridor. Mr. Turner took one last glance at Mr. Lee before hurrying away.

Mr. Clayton stared at Mr. Carter with a look of distress. "It never should have come to this," he said.

"No, it shouldn't have," Mr. Carter agreed. "Now, go."

Mr. Clayton shook his head, slowly turning and following after the other two.

Mr. McDonough took a hesitant step toward Mr. Carter, and opened his mouth to speak before Mr. Carter held up his hand. "I'm sorry, old friend. I cannot trust even you right now."

"I understand how troubled you must be by this, but I can assure you – " he began.

"Troubled?" Mr. Carter asked, aghast. "How could you possibly understand what – "

"I understand better than you know," Mr. McDonough interrupted. "In fact, the three of us do. I told you about the death that occurred on the ship coming over from New York, yes?"

Mr. Carter turned to glance at Felix and I. "They were on that ship with you?"

Mr. McDonough nodded. "We must do what we can to remain calm right now. If you allow your anger or fear to get the best of you, I can promise that you will regret it. You need a clear mind until this matter is resolved. Can I at least persuade you to agree with that?"

Mr. Carter turned the blade over in his hand, and for a wild moment, I thought he might lash out at Mr. McDonough with it. "I will do what I can," Mr. Carter said. He turned to look at Mr. Lee. "Why him? Why now of all times?"

"I do not know," Mr. McDonough said. "But one thing we can be certain of...the men who are here are no longer playing games, my friend. They mean to end this, one way or the other."

"I'm afraid you're right," Mr. Carter said, his expression hardening. "What should I do?"

"Do as you said you would," Mr. McDonough said. "And do not give them a single inch until we find out who did this."

Not an inch...and perhaps we can all make it out of this alive.

9

"My dear, you have been awfully quiet about all this..." Mr. Carter said, turning to his wife a moment later, taking her hand in his. "I would like for you to tell me what you are thinking."

"Oh, darling, I thought – I thought the worst had happened," Mrs. Carter said, grabbing hold of his arms, squeezing tightly. "I thought I had found *you* out here in the hall, lying there – "

"Me?" Mr. Carter asked. "My word, why did you think it was me?"

Mrs. Carter's sobs returned, and she gave him a shove with the heel of her palm against his chest. "Oh, you *fool*!" she cried before burying her face against his chest again. "All these threats that have been sent to our home, our children being followed, the brick through the window!" She stood up straight again, searching his face, her tears reflecting the bright light of the candles in the candelabra still held by the butler. "How can you possibly think they are not targeting you?"

"Well, it isn't me who lies dead at our feet," Mr. Carter said.

"Oh, never mind..." she said, angry tears still spilling from her eyes. "You will never listen to me. I – I must go to the children again." She pushed his hands away, and started back down the hall, away from the corpse, into the darkness.

"She has a point, sir," Felix said a moment later, after she had departed. "If I may."

Mr. Carter turned to look at Felix, and his gaze hardened. "I believe I asked everyone to start making their way to the drawing room again."

"It's all right, Carter, you can trust them," Mr. McDonough said. "You have my word."

The look in Mr. Carter's eyes suggested he did not fully believe Mr. McDonough, but he pursed his lips tightly shut.

"How well did you know Mr. Lee?" I asked.

"I don't see how this is any of your business," Mr. Carter said. He turned to look at the butler. "Lewis, find one of the young men and send him out to fetch the police. We don't have any time to waste."

Lewis nodded, and leaving the candelabra on one of the narrow hall tables, started off through the darkness.

"Your wife is right in asking," Mr. McDonough asked. "What if your associates are trying to send a much stronger message?"

"Attack Mr. Lee in order to change my mind?" Mr. Carter asked. His expression became somber. "I don't know if that makes a great deal of sense. Wouldn't they have gone after someone else?"

Mr. McDonough shrugged. "There must be a reason why they chose him."

Mr. McDonough was right. For whatever reason, Mr. Lee had been in the wrong place at the wrong time.

It isn't as if this could really have been premeditated, could it? There is no way anyone could have predicted that the storm would be so bad as to strand us all here this evening, nor that the power would also go out. It seems as if someone felt pushed to quick action, resulting in an act that was hasty and ill-planned. After all, the killer's very presence in the house makes him a known suspect. Who would choose to implicate himself in such a way?

"Well, whatever their reason may be, I don't intend to leave them alone to find another reason to lash out," Mr. Carter said, snatching the candelabra off the table and starting down the hall. "I'll have to keep an eye on them all, lest – "

Lewis had reappeared, looking worried.

"What's the matter?" Mr. Carter asked. "What else could possibly have gone wrong now?"

"I am sorry, sir, but there is no way to get anyone immediately through to the police," Lewis said. "The rains are too heavy, the streets so dangerously flooded that it would risk the messenger's life."

"Very well," Mr. Carter said, sounding reluctant and weary. "But make sure that the moment someone is able to go, the moment the streets are clear, someone must set out. We cannot simply leave a dead body lying in the floor..."

He had reached the open doorway to the drawing

room, and the moment he entered, Mr. Ward's voice carried out like an ebbing tide. "Mr. Carter, we have come to a conclusion."

"What sort of conclusion is this?" Mr. Carter asked, suspiciously.

I stepped up to the doorway as Mr. McDonough followed Mr. Carter in, Felix lingering there beside me.

Mr. Ward stood near the fireplace, Mr. Turner sitting in one of the chairs beside him. Mr. Clayton had given himself some space from the other two men, standing and gazing down at the game of cards lying forgotten on the round table along the wall.

Mr. Ward seemed to be the speaker for the group, as the other two chose to remain silent. The sneer spreading across Mr. Ward's face could only have been rivaled by the one that Mr. Lee had worn earlier that evening. The thought sent shivers down my spine. *The man was alive so recently...and now he is gone, unpleasant though he was.*

"You thought you could fool us, didn't you, Carter?" Mr. Ward asked. "Bringing us all here, finding a way to keep us in the house, and then murdering Mr. Lee?"

"Are you really going to stand there and accuse me of this?" Mr. Carter asked with a rather nasty laugh. "I knew that you were a fool, Ward, but to go to such lengths?"

"Me going to such lengths?" Mr. Ward asked, his voice layered in sarcasm and astonishment. "What of you? We know how sour things had become between you and Mr. Lee. You are the only one who could have taken his life."

Mr. Carter opened his mouth to speak, but hesitated.

My heart skipped. That was quite the accusation, and yet Mr. Carter did not react the way I thought he might; angered, outraged, appalled. Instead, he said nothing.

"I knew it..." Mr. Turner said, his forehead wrinkling, eyes narrowing to slits as he adjusted his glasses once more up the bridge of his slightly crooked nose.

"You know as well as I that I did not kill Mr. Lee," Mr. Carter said, an edge to his words. "That being said...you are not incorrect in saying that things had been tense between us as of late."

An expression of triumph crossed Mr. Ward's face. "Well, well...I'd say what we have right here, gentlemen, is a motive for murder."

Mr. Carter frowned, and he made it a point to wave the sword a bit as his side as he rolled his shoulders, as if to remind his guests of whose house they were in.

Although I understood that he was in a stressful situation, I eyed that sword and worried that the circumstances might be pushing him to the brink of doing something foolish. What sort of host brandished a weapon at his guests and kept them hostage in his drawing room?

Then again, this is hardly a typical situation...I only hope that he doesn't turn on Felix and I next.

"Since it seems that our dear host here does not wish to share with everyone precisely what I am referring to, why don't I enlighten you all?" Mr. Ward suggested to the rest of us. "This all began about three weeks ago. I am certain that my associates here will remember what I am referencing simply by the timeframe alone, but for those of you less acquainted with the goings on when Mr. Carter attends business meetings, allow me to fill you in."

He began to pace back and forth in front of the fireplace, his hands clasped neatly behind his back.

A nasty shiver ran down the base of my spine, and

while I knew that for the good of our investigation I should hear what he had to say, I still could not quite shake the feeling that Mr. Ward was enjoying this pointing of fingers at Mr. Carter far too much.

"It was on this day, the second Thursday of the month, when we were to have one of our meetings to discuss various matters," Mr. Ward began. "After the meeting was over, Mr. Carter pulled Mr. Lee aside to speak with him, and Mr. Lee obliged like the sensible man he was."

Even I knew that was an inaccurate description of the deceased, and I hardly knew the man.

"Raised voices and shouts could quickly be heard down the hall as Mr. Clayton, Mr. Turner, and I, along with some others were gathering our belongings and starting to make our way out of the building."

"You have no idea what it is you are talking about," Mr. Carter spat, taking a step toward Mr. Ward. "You did not hear what started that conversation – "

"I did not need to," Mr. Ward said with a hollow laugh. "What else is there to know apart from the fact that it very nearly came to blows? It certainly would have, if I had not walked in to break things up."

"I will admit that we had a disagreement on matters of business. I had been trying to talk Mr. Lee out of some decision, but you all truly do not know the sort of dealings he had, how dastardly he really was."

"That doesn't prove your innocence, Carter," Mr. Ward said. "You are still the only one who had any real issue with the man."

"I have told you, I did not kill him!"

"But how can you prove that?" Mr. Ward demanded.

"In such a dark place, without anyone seeing you! Can anyone account for your whereabouts in the few minutes before his death?"

"My butler can," Mr. Carter said.

"Your butler's word means nothing," Mr. Ward said. "It will mean even less to the police when they – "

"Enough!"

To my great surprise, Mr. McDonough stepped up between the two arguing men, his arms outstretched as if anticipating an all out fight between the pair.

"You must both calm your tempers," he said. "We cannot afford for this night to descend into chaos any more than it already has. Given the inability for the police to be sent for, and the rains keeping us hostage here, we have no choice but to all reside underneath the same roof tonight, and – "

"This is ridiculous, man, get out of the way!" Mr. Ward barked.

"No, you listen to me," Mr. McDonough said. "There is a corpse lying out in the hall, in case you have forgotten."

"That is *precisely* what we are on about!" Mr. Ward hollered. "Have you not been following?"

"All I am hearing is you all trying to push blame around," Felix said. "It is plain that you are dancing around the issue, instead of dealing with it directly."

Mr. Ward turned his angered gaze upon Felix. "No one has asked *you* to interfere with our business."

Felix met his glare with one of his own. "I think this matter concerns any and all of us present this evening," he said. "You are not the only one."

"It certainly does concern us all," Mr. Ward said, eyes

narrowing. "Perhaps you know something that you would care to share with the rest of us?"

Felix shook his head. "I know nothing that you do not already know."

"Enough," Mr. Carter interjected, storming off back toward the door. "I am going to have my staff watch the door, along with any other exits to the house. You would do well not to try and leave before the authorities arrive."

"Where are you going?" Mr. Clayton asked.

"I will check all the doors and windows for signs of forced entry and ensure there is no intruder lingering anywhere in the house," Mr. Carter said. "I don't believe for one moment that the killing was a random robbery attempt, but I must rule out the possibility the attacker came from outside. As for the rest of you, you will remain in here. Lewis, I need you to stand by the door there. Do not allow anyone out for any reason."

The dignified butler looked a bit startled, most likely at the suggestion he could physically prevent a group of men from pushing out of the room if they chose to. Still, he nodded loyally. If anyone got past him, it seemed they would not do so without meeting resistance.

Mr. Carter shot one last infuriated stare around the room at the rest of the guests before striding out into the hall, his footsteps disappearing after him in the darkness.

"This is something we all need to be taking very seriously," Mr. McDonough said. "I will also remain here, so as to keep an eye on you all."

"*Someone* is certainly eager to gain Carter's favor, perhaps to paint himself as an ally and not a suspect?" Mr. Ward muttered.

Mr. McDonough didn't bother to argue, but instead

looked over at Felix and me. "What will you do?" he asked quietly.

"Perhaps my brother and I should go and see about Mrs. Carter," I said.

She and her husband could really use our services about now.

"Very well," Mr. McDonough said. "Be careful. As our host said, there is no telling what dangers might lurk in the rest of the house."

"Wait, you are going to allow them to leave?" Mr. Turner asked, getting to his feet.

"They were here in the room when Mr. Lee was found dead," Mr. McDonough pointed out. "Above anyone else in this house, I know full well that the pair of them are innocent. So yes, I am going to allow them to leave."

Felix said nothing else, slipping out into the hall.

I, however, took a moment of selfish pleasure in strolling leisurely out of the room as I left them to rot in their prison under the watchful eyes of Mr. McDonough and the butler.

"You really think it wise to make enemies so soon?" Felix asked.

"It matters very little, brother," I said. "I have a feeling they were all our enemies from the start."

10

I didn't take us long to overhear the frantic voices of Mr. and Mrs. Carter speaking in what I imagined they thought to be hushed tones. They had barricaded themselves in the dining room on the opposite side of the house, and we were intercepted by a young servant who stepped in front of us as we approached.

"Mr. Carter has asked not to be disturbed," he said.

"Yes, but Mrs. Carter has hired us for an important task," I said. "If you would please allow us the chance to – "

He sidestepped in front of me as I started toward the door. "I am sorry, Miss, but he was quite clear."

"You do not understand," I said. "My brother and I are – "

"It is of vital importance that we speak to Mrs. Carter," Felix said, interrupting me. "Trust me. She will agree. You can ask her, if you wish."

The servant's eyes widened. "What are your names?"

"Mr. and Miss Crawford," Felix said.

The servant took a hesitant glance over his shoulder before slowly approaching the door. He opened it, and the voices within quieted as he ducked his head inside.

A moment later, he withdrew and looked over his shoulder at us before waving us over.

Mrs. Carter clasped her hands together as I entered the dining room, Felix right behind me. "Oh, I had *hoped* you would come and find me," she said. "How could I have possibly known that all of this would happen?"

"It's all right, Mrs. Carter," Felix said. "We are here to help."

Mr. Carter's expression hardened from behind his wife. The sword he had been brandishing at Mr. Ward lay at an odd angle across the table, as if he'd thrown it across. "You both should be waiting in the drawing room with the others," he said. "How did you find your way out?"

"Mr. McDonough let us go," I said.

Mr. Carter shook his head, flicking his wrist toward the door. "No. You need to leave."

"Darling, no," Mrs. Carter said, grabbing hold of the elbow of his shirt. "You see...I hired them."

"Hired them?" Mr. Carter asked. "What do you mean?"

She looked forlornly up at him, her already puffy eyes welling with tears once again. "I hired them to come and investigate the threats we have been receiving."

"You did what?" Mr. Carter asked, sounding breathless, as if all the air had been snatched from his lungs. He sank down into one of the dining room chairs beside him. "Without consulting me at all?"

"You would not listen to reason," she said, lowering

herself into the chair beside him, laying her hands on his knees. "Every time I asked you to take the matter to the authorities, you simply refused."

"I have had it under control this entire time," Mr. Carter said, brow furrowing. "The threatening notes were nothing more than bluffs – "

"I think tonight can prove differently, Mr. Carter," I said.

He shot me a nasty look.

"My dear, I am afraid," Mrs. Carter said. "Terrified. Mr. Lee is *dead*, and I feel sure it is all connected to the threats and this entire affair with the business plans."

"Do you think I should relent?" Mr. Carter asked.

"It wouldn't do you any good to do so now," I said. "The lines have been drawn, and you've made enemies."

Mr. Carter let his head fall against his hand, rubbing his hairline, as if trying to massage away what was sure to be a terrible headache coming on.

"We cannot do anything until the police arrive," he said, slamming his palm flat against the table, a sound which made Mrs. Carter jump in her seat. "They will be able to sort this out."

"I wouldn't place too much confidence in the authorities," I said, wrinkling my nose. "Do you know how long it will take them to discover who is responsible for the murder, if they ever do? They have many of these sorts of cases, some of which simply never get solved. No...my brother and I are your best bet at finding out who did this before it's too late."

Mr. Carter looked up at us, his forehead wrinkling further. "Just who are you?"

"We are private detectives, sir," Felix said. "Your wife came to us in order to protect you."

Mr. Carter looked at her, stunned. "Private detectives? You told me we met them at a charity dinner."

"I know, darling, I'm sorry..." she said, dabbing away at more tears with a blue handkerchief. "I just – I just wanted to make sure that you were safe."

Mr. Carter sighed heavily, shaking his head.

"For what it's worth, Mr. McDonough can vouch for us," I said. "We solved a murder aboard the ship we were all on some weeks ago, the incident he mentioned to you?"

A light appeared behind Mr. Carter's eyes, and for the first time, I recognized hope, though it was buried down deep, and dim. "He told me of that tragedy, yes..." he said in a small voice.

"My dear, please let them help us," Mrs. Carter said. "I cannot stand any of this for one more *minute.*"

Mr. Carter looked up at me, and then Felix. "My apologies for being so cross with you," he said, the muscles in his jaw working. "What can I do to help?"

"You could provide us with some more information," I said. "First of all about your relationship with Mr. Lee, and why Mr. Ward is so insistent that you killed Lee."

Our host's anger returned swiftly. "You think that I did this?"

"Probably not," I said, meeting his firm gaze with one of my own. "However, I am going to need to know the truth, the *full* truth, so that we can exonerate you."

"The more we know, the easier it will make it for us to find who committed the crime," Felix said.

Mr. Carter looked apologetically up at his wife before drawing in another deep breath through his nose. "Very well," he said. "As I said back in the drawing room, Mr. Lee and I have known one another for quite some time, though more recently, things have been rather...rocky."

"Why is that?" I asked.

"Mr. Lee was...well, he was not the sort that I liked to have over for a meal with my family, let me say that," he said. "Something had changed in him over the years, as when we had all agreed to admit him to the company board several years ago, he had seemed perfectly agreeable at the time. He had agreed to all of our bylaws and standards, which are meant to hold our business practices accountable. Over time, I heard rumors that he had begun to take on some less than savory business deals, but when confronted, he simply denied it. No one else wanted his dismissal, which led me to think that everyone else had secrets of their own that they didn't want discovered. It was at this point that I realized just how corrupt everything had become, and in my care and supervision. I felt responsible."

"Darling, you are too hard on yourself..." Mrs. Carter said.

He shook his head. "No. I see now that I have been a fool, thinking everyone I worked with was trustworthy. I should have known a man can quite easily say one thing and do something else entirely different."

I could see the hurt in Mrs. Carter's face as she watched him relate his new understandings.

"So matters nearly came to blows?" I asked.

Mr. Carter exhaled sharply. "It very nearly did," he

said. "It is not my proudest moment, but I had realized that no amount of talking was going to convince Mr. Lee his decisions were damaging to the company and everyone we employed. And now...now we are brought to this situation." He frowned. "Speaking of which, Miss Crawford, I cannot seem to make sense of what you thought earlier." He looked at me.

"What I thought?" I asked.

"You suggested he was killed as a means of targeting me," Mr. Carter said. "All of my associates knew that Mr. Lee and I had not been getting on. In fact, I cannot even say that I am terribly grieved that he is dead."

"Darling!" Mrs. Carter said, sounding aghast.

He shrugged. "If ever there was a deserving victim, a man whose greed had harmed many people, it was Mr. Lee. But why target him?"

"That's what we aim to figure out," I said. "Which does lead me to wonder about what happened this evening. Mrs. Carter, I am sorry, but I must ask you what you can remember about finding Mr. Lee when you did."

Mrs. Carter looked distressed.

Her husband reached out and took hold of one of her hands. "It's all right, my dear. I am right here with you."

She gave him a grateful smile. "Well...I was...I was on my way to inform the guests that rooms were being prepared for them to stay the night in, and I – " She quickly pinched her eyes closed, and covered her mouth with her free hand. "I'm sorry," she went on a moment later. "The thought of it, all over again..."

"We understand," Felix said. "But anything you can remember could be helpful."

She nodded. "I...nearly stumbled over Mr. Lee. I know my home, after all. I didn't need a light, as I didn't fear traversing it in the dark. I knew the candles needed to be used sparingly, if we were going to use them all night. And of course, who would have expected someone to be – to be lying on the floor in the middle of the corridor?"

"No one could expect it, of course," I said. "Do you remember anything strange? Anything out of place?"

"No," Mrs. Carter said. "But I was in such a state of shock in that moment, I took in very few details, if I'm honest."

"Well..." I said, looking up at Felix. "What do you think?"

"I suspect our culprit is sitting beneath the watch of our friend Mr. McDonough," he said.

"As do I," I said. "Though I do not suppose, Mr. Carter, that you've encountered any signs of a forced entry from outside, anything to indicate an intruder crept into the house?"

"None as of yet, and I don't expect to," he said. "I regret to say the killer is most likely one of our own guests."

I nodded. "We will find out who did this, don't you worry, either of you."

"You know..." Mr. Carter said. "I begin to wonder if someone killed Mr. Lee in order to frame me. Mr. Ward seems all too ready to blame me, with the story about our past argument, and his knowledge of our dislike for each other."

"That's not a bad theory," Felix said. "However, it's clear that such an accusation against you would not hold water when examined closely. You can rest assured about that."

"If one of those men killed him..." I said. "It should not be too terribly difficult to discover which of them it was."

11

"I am a bit reluctant to return to the drawing room," I said as Felix and I made our way back down the hall, with a silver candlestick in hand. Mrs. Carter had not wanted us to walk the halls in the dark all alone.

"Why?" Felix asked.

"I just have a bad feeling about all this..." I said. "Something tells me the situation is only going to get worse."

"Well, you aren't wrong about that," Felix said. "I am feeling the same. Still...maybe its better not to drag it all out for days like we have in the past."

"That wasn't without trying to end things as quickly as possible," I said. "We've always tried to work quickly."

"That isn't what I meant," Felix said. "All I mean is that it could be for the best."

"What will we do if we succeed in uncovering the killer's identity?" I asked. "Shall we throw the culprit into a room, lock the door, and wait for morning? How can we know that he won't fly into a mad rage and try to attack everyone within reach, before he can be restrained?"

Felix's brow furrowed. "I don't know. We haven't really been in this situation before, have we?"

"Not in a place where we haven't been able to contact the police, we haven't," I said.

We reached the drawing room and found the butler standing outside the doors, just as the other servant had near the dining room.

"You've returned," Lewis said.

"Yes, we spoke with Mr. and Mrs. Carter, and they fared well enough," I said.

"They're quite safe," Felix added. "Mr. Carter is comforting Mrs. Carter, in the dining room."

Lewis nodded, but the wrinkles remained deeply carved into his forehead. "Mr. Carter must trust you both, to allow you complete access to the house. Therefore, I shall do the same. I must warn you, however, that if you do anything against my master, you shall be dealt with...appropriately."

My eyes widened. "Well, I am pleased to hear Mr. Carter has such excellent protection," I said. "Let's hope you do not have to test that courage of yours."

That seemed to surprise him, for I saw a flash of fear in his eyes. Most likely, he had not considered exactly how far he might need to go in protection of the Carter family.

"Lewis, we need to get into the drawing room," Felix said. "We have some things to ask those gentlemen inside."

"Is that wise?" he asked.

"We will know soon enough," I said. "Has anyone been sent yet to fetch the police?"

Lewis shook his head. "No. I had someone check mere minutes ago; it is still like a hurricane out there; it has only gotten darker and the rains more torrential."

I nodded. "The thunder made me think as much." As if on cue, more of it clapped overhead.

I winced. I knew that come morning, my head was sure to be throbbing.

Lewis pulled open the door for us, and Felix and I stepped inside.

It should not have surprised me that the room was divided as it was, but I still found it rather interesting to see Mr. Ward, Mr. Turner, and Mr. Clayton all standing in the far corner, their heads bent together as they spoke in hushed tones. Mr. McDonough, on the other hand, sat in a chair nearest to the door, with a full view of the room.

He noticed us as we came in, and quickly hopped out of his seat.

"If you have left and come back, then I can only imagine there is one reason for it," Mr. McDonough said in a low voice. He turned away from the group in the corner, where I noticed Mr. Ward shifting his gaze in our direction. "Earlier this week, I saw an advertisement in the paper, and while I did not imagine the name Crawford could have referred to the two of you, I am now starting to doubt myself."

"That was our advertisement, yes," I said.

He nodded. "If you've been hired to act as detectives for the Carters, then I can only imagine your intentions are going to be to question everyone until someone confesses, but allow me to implore you to keep your purpose secret until you absolutely cannot do so any longer."

"You mean, don't tell anyone we are investigators?" Felix asked.

"Precisely," Mr. McDonough said through tight lips. "If these men guess at your intentions, they will tell you nothing."

My eyes narrowed. "How clever you are, Mr. McDonough, to be able to discern our plans," I said. "It is fortunate that you do not find yourself among the suspects this time."

His mouth twitched at one corner, and I sensed he was trying to judge whether I was serious. "I could not agree more," he said. "It is a pleasant change to find myself above suspicion."

"Oh, I shouldn't say that," I said. "Is anyone ever really above suspicion?"

He glanced at Felix. "You both know I was speaking with you at the time of the murder," he pointed out.

"Lillian, stop trying to unnerve Mr. McDonough," Felix agreed. "We have already determined him to be an ally."

"True enough," I admitted, and glanced at the men gathered nearby. "I can only hope that whoever killed Mr. Lee will be less astute than you, sir."

"I do not think you have anything to fear...yet," Mr. McDonough said. "The story that you both have woven tonight should be the one you stick with, and maybe you will be able to get someone to talk."

"Perhaps..." Felix said. "Though it is obvious they trust us about as much as they trust you."

"Yes, that is true," he said. "But they have all been

spooked now. Mr. Lee's death has thrown everyone off kilter."

"Even the person responsible," I said. "Unless someone is a very good actor."

"I have found that one cannot be both diplomatic and a good actor," Mr. McDonough said. "You develop one skill over the other."

"Interesting," I said, glaring out over the rest of the room. "So it seems that for the moment, we have the upper hand."

"You very well might," Mr. McDonough said. "For the time being."

"So, what do you suggest?" I asked.

"I think we need to get what information we can, perhaps change our tactic from being against them to standing with them," Felix said.

I shook my head. "That's not going to work. They are going to see right through our efforts."

"Maybe," Mr. McDonough said.

"What if they know something about Mr. Carter that we don't know?" Felix asked.

I looked up at him. "Are you thinking he is possibly lying to us? Because I tend to believe what he said."

"I do as well..." Felix said, dropping his voice, also turning away from some of the glances Mr. Turner now seemed to be sending our way. "But that doesn't mean we can't try to convince *them* that we don't believe him any longer."

I nodded. "I suppose the best we can do is try. For now, we need to collect more information before we can make any accusations."

"Good," Mr. McDonough said. "That seems a sound plan."

"Come on, then," I said to Felix. "We might as well go get this over with."

I started across the room, and immediately the three men on the other end quieted.

"Well, well...if it isn't the Crawfords," Mr. Turner said, glaring at us from behind his spectacles. "What's the matter? Come to tell us off again."

"No, on the contrary," Felix said. "We have come to share in your frustrations."

"Indeed," I said. "Something suspicious seems to be going on, and I do not much care for it."

Mr. Ward snorted. "You and that McDonough have been in cahoots with Carter from the beginning. What makes you think we will trust you after what you've told us?"

"We cannot make you trust us," Felix said. "But the fact is our father sent my sister and me to England as a means of finding information about various businesses here in London, places he might wish to make international investments in. He hopes we may form some...advantageous connections during our time here."

"We are all too happy to make any connections we can," I added. "Not merely with Mr. Carter."

Mr. Ward's eyes, as hard as steel, did not waver.

Mr. Turner, though, sniffed with derision at us. "Oh, *now* you want help," he said. "What, have you realized what a liar Carter is?"

"We certainly are learning that not everything is as it seems to be," I said generously. "What can you tell us about Mr. Carter that we don't know?"

Mr. Turner laughed. "Oh, he is the last man anyone should trust. He *claims* that the changes he wants are for the good of the company, but I know he has something up his sleeve, some scheme or other..."

"Oh, really?" I asked. "What, exactly, is he planning?"

Mr. Turner snapped his jaw closed quickly. "We haven't figured that out yet, but we are trying to," he said. "There has to be some reason why he has been making these ridiculous decisions as of late – "

"Turner..." Mr. Ward said in a low voice. "You would do well to watch precisely what you say in front of our new acquaintances."

"Oh, come now, Mr. Ward," I said. "We are all in the business of money here, aren't we? What makes you think that you have us figured out so quickly?"

Mr. Ward's eyes flashed, and he said nothing else.

"If you have any sense about you, you will not allow yourselves to get too close to Carter," Mr. Turner said, his glasses slipping down the bridge of his nose. "He is unsuitable to be the leader of the company, and a poor name for you to take back to share with your father."

Yet no one seems to be able to provide a decent answer as to why...nothing that really makes sense, anyway.

"Mr. Clayton, what of your thoughts?" Felix asked. "You have been awfully quiet about all this."

Mr. Clayton stood with his mouth downturned, and his eyes fixed on some spot on the floor. "There isn't much to say..." he said. "I cannot understand why anyone wants to discuss anything apart from what happened to Lee."

"That is what we are discussing," Mr. Turner snapped.

"Is it, though?" I asked. "Tell me, what of Mr. Lee? Why was he killed?"

"Carter did it, I am certain of it," Mr. Ward said through clenched teeth.

"Yes, yes it was him!" Mr. Turner exclaimed.

Mr. Clayton looked up. "I am still not convinced – "

"Well, it wasn't I, was it, Clayton?" Mr. Ward snapped. "Nor Mr. Turner. So who else could it have been? Who else would have had the motive?"

I realized what they were doing. They were trying to persuade Mr. Clayton to go over to their side, so they might act as a unified force when the time eventually came to be interviewed by the police. They hoped their numbers would outweigh Mr. Carter's word.

But what if it was Mr. Clayton?

We needed to separate them. We had heard Mr. Carter's tale, but these men fed off one another's word. And Mr. Ward...he seemed to control them all, seemed to lead the charge.

I needed the other two away from him before I would be able to hear what they *really* thought about Mr. Lee or Mr. Carter.

12

"If you gentlemen do not mind, I must excuse myself for a moment," I said. "Felix, if you would come with me, please? Something has just come to mind, and I wish to discuss it with you before we offer it to the others."

Felix looked down at me and nodded. "Certainly. If it is the same thing I am considering, I imagine this could prove advantageous to our efforts."

"Your efforts? What efforts?" Mr. Turner asked, his eyes closing to slits.

"Oh, don't you worry, Mr. Turner. When we let you know, I am sure you will be most surprised," Felix said. "It could prove to be quite beneficial."

Mr. Turner's eyes lit up. "Well...when you say it that way – "

"Are you talking of a business deal?" Mr. Ward asked.

"Perhaps," I said. "Come along, Felix. Let us go and discuss the matter at hand."

I started off toward the door once more, Felix close behind.

It wasn't until we were out in the hall that I spoke up again.

"We need to separate them," I said.

"As I expected, we are of the same mind," Felix said. "Mr. Ward seems to hold the reins on the others. It is no surprise that he is the one with the most mistrust toward Mr. Carter."

"Indeed," I said. "Which is why we must get the real story. There is no other way that we will be able to find why someone killed Mr. Lee, who I am beginning to think more than not was nothing more than a means to an end."

"It's unfortunate to think in such a way, but I believe you might be right," Felix said. "With how little regard anyone seems to be paying his death, I think he may have been seen as expendable."

I wrinkled my nose. "While I don't wish for anyone's death, I must admit I can see *why* he garnered so little respect from his colleagues, and as such, has attracted little of their concern in his death."

Felix shrugged. "No doubt," he said. "So...how should we go about this?"

It took some arguing, but we settled upon a logical way to separate them all. In the end, I decided to speak with Mr. Clayton, while Felix would speak with Mr. Turner. Mr. McDonough would remain in the room with Mr. Ward. "No sense in either of you dealing with him if he is the most mistrusting of the lot," McDonough said when we had brought the idea to him. "You have a better chance of getting something out of the others."

I knew that our cover would soon be blown, sepa-
rating them the way we were. Felix, along with some of
the servants Lewis had sent for, went with Mr. Turner to
the parlor near the front door, while Lewis led Mr.
Clayton and me to the study just next door to the
drawing room. I could only hope our suspects would see
this more as the staff being careful to follow the Carters'
orders, rather than the staff showing favoritism or coop-
eration to my brother and me.

"Well, now, aren't we all a great deal more like prisoners than guests?" Mr. Clayton asked as Lewis closed
the door behind the pair of us.

Looking at him, I realized that he looked a great
deal like one of my father's friends from back home.
Mr. Ranford. I rather liked Mr. Ranford, as well as his
children whom I played with when I was much
younger. He had always been kind to me, if a bit stoic
and dull.

As Clayton stared at me, his arms folded tightly
across himself, I noticed something in his gaze...some-
thing that had not been there before.

*No, that's not true...it was there...but now it isn't veiled as
it was.*

"Not prisoners, I'd say," I began. "Mr. Carter is just
being wisely cautious."

"And Mr. Ward was right," Mr. Clayton said. "You and
your brother and that McDonough are all working with
Carter."

I shook my head. "No, we aren't working *with*
anyone," I said. "We operate under our own rules. Mr.
Carter was simply the connection we had to your
company."

Mr. Clayton's brow furrowed. "Yet there must be a reason why you have separated us like this," he said.

I knew that our façade was growing rather thin, and if we wanted to find the truth, we were going to have to evade suspicion for a short time longer. "I think Mr. Carter is worried that someone else is going to be harmed," I said.

"Then why not ensure we are all in solitary rooms?" Mr. Clayton asked. "Why is it that you are the ones deciding who goes where?"

"Mr. Clayton..." I said, a bit sharper than I likely needed to be.

I wished Felix were here, as he always seemed to handle these sorts of conversations better than I did. He, and Eugene.

I suppose I had best do what I can to follow their lead, and keep a cool temper as they would.

I took a deep breath, trying to soothe the impatience swelling up inside me.

"This night has been very stressful on all of us," I began, much slower, much more gently. "Surely, we are all hoping to find the answers we are looking for. This whole fiasco has unsettled everyone, and all we want is to be able to go home."

Mr. Clayton shifted back and forth on his feet, averting his eyes to the long row of shelves along the wall. Mr. Carter, it seemed, was quite fond of books about economics, given the titles lining the rows. "You are not wrong," he said.

"I saw nothing, nor did my brother," I said, sinking down into one of the chairs, perhaps exaggerating my exasperation a bit more than necessary, playing it up as a means of keeping him distracted. "I wish we had, then maybe we would already know who killed Mr. Lee, and it could have been handled however Mr. Carter saw fit..." I shook my head. "But who knows what that would even look like?"

Mr. Clayton rubbed the back of his neck. "The police will have to deal with whoever did this when they are able to arrive."

"But who knows when that will be?" I asked, pointing toward the window. "Goodness knows the weather doesn't seem to want to clear up."

"It won't last forever," Mr. Clayton said.

I allowed my head to fall into my hands. "What if they never find the killer?" I asked, taking on a desperate tone.

I heard footsteps, and I had to resist the urge to grin into my hands. *Look at that. I'm not so terrible an actress after all.*

"You must be around the same age as my daughter..." Mr. Clayton said. "There is no reason why anyone as young as you should have to endure such terrible things. I am sorry that you happened to be here this evening. It... it never should have happened."

I lifted my eyes, making sure to keep them as wide and child-like as possible. "Do you know anything?" I asked.

"About Mr. Lee?" he asked. "N – No. I know no more than any of the rest..." He frowned. "Though I know that someone in this house is clearly capable of shocking things."

"Yes...but who?" I asked.

"I must admit that I am not terribly surprised Mr. Lee has met his end in this way," Mr. Clayton said in a low voice. "Not that I expected him to – well, for what happened tonight to happen. Not here, not now...but eventually, I assumed he would anger someone enough that they would come after him."

He glanced around, as if to reassure himself that we remained alone, before continuing. "Mr. Lee was involved in so many questionable dealings with shady characters, of late. Which is precisely what had upset Mr. Carter so much...and to be honest...it unsettled me, as well. These were not the sorts of clients I would ever associate with, but I had known Mr. Lee for years, so that made his actions seem...tolerable." He grimaced. "Looking back, none of it should ever have been acceptable."

"So, he was the only one who had these sorts of tendencies?" I asked. "The only one who dabbled in risky businesses ventures with untrustworthy clients?"

"Well...this has made me question what I really know of these men I have worked alongside for so long," Mr. Clayton said.

"Really?" I asked, raising my eyebrows encouragingly.

Interesting. There's no knowing if he's being truthful or merely trying to make himself seem more honorable than the rest, but let's see how far he is willing to betray the others.

He raked his fingers over his cheek, his eyes hollow and vacant. "Take Mr. Ward, for instance," he said. "I know for certain that he has been pinching money from the company account, calling it his *due payment* for Mr. Carter being what he considered stingy." He shook his head, his face paling. "The worst part is...I have agreed with him. Knowing what it has led to now, however...I don't know what to think about any of this."

If he is not sincere, he is a good actor...

"I suppose I can understand why Mr. Ward has been fighting Mr. Carter's decision so much, then," I said. "He is worried Mr. Carter's proposed changes to the business will expose his actions."

"Precisely," Mr. Clayton said. "I thought Carter was entirely wrong for wanting to change things...now Mr. Lee ends up dead, and I can only imagine that it is because of this argument. It became too great. It – it spun entirely out of control..."

He turned and started off toward the window. Rain continued to pelt the glass, streaking down like veins in stone.

"I have trouble thinking this, but I – " he said.

This is it. He is teetering, right there on the edge of realizing the depth of the issue. He just needs a small, gentle push –

"It would be a shame for the company to fall apart, simply because one man allowed his emotions to get the better of him," I said. "Allowed his hatred to boil over, leading him to kill someone once considered a friend."

"...You're right," Mr. Clayton said.

"I don't think anyone can stress enough the severity of this whole situation," I said. "I can only hope that whoever did it will come forward, and confess their crime. Otherwise, Mr. Lee will have no justice."

Mr. Clayton's shoulders stiffened, and he stared at his reflection, or what little of it he might have seen in the pale light of the candles in the room. "I cannot stand idly by any longer..." he said. He turned around. "I think Mr. Ward is responsible."

Finally!

I cautioned myself not to become too excited. An

accusation with little to back it up meant nothing, but it was certainly a good starting place.

"Mr. Ward?" I asked, trying to sound appalled. "Really?"

"Come, now, you might not know the man well, but surely you have seen enough of his character tonight to see why I can blame him," Mr. Clayton said. "He has little care for anyone apart from himself. I think tonight has proved it."

I rose from my seat. "Well, Mr. Clayton...let's hope that you are right, so that we may put this whole ordeal behind us."

Mr. Clayton nodded.

"If we confront him all together, he will have nowhere to hide," I said, smoothing my hands over the front of my dress. "If guilty, he will have no choice but to confess. So why don't we go and do just that?"

He lost even more color from his face. "Confront – confront him? Do you really think that wise?"

"What can he possibly do to harm us, if there are more of us than him?" I asked.

Mr. Clayton shook his head. "He – he may very well have *killed* Mr. Lee! What makes you think he won't try and do the same to the rest of us?"

"We have the advantage," I said. "We *must* confront him before anything worse happens. Mr. Clayton, there are *children* sleeping upstairs. Do you really think we should simply let this lie until the weather clears and the police can be brought in?"

"What – what do you suggest we do?" he asked, rubbing his hand over his face, his arm shaking.

"You find your courage, Mr. Clayton," I said, eyes hardening. "For you will be of little help until you do."

Mr. Clayton swallowed, searched my face for a moment, and then nodded. His hand at his side balled into a tight fist. "Very well," he said. "I will – I will do what I can."

"Very good," I said. "Let us go and see what can be done."

I informed Lewis that we would like to return to my brother, and he agreed to accompany us back to the drawing room. We lingered out in the hall, however, knowing that Mr. Ward lay on the other side of the door, like a snake waiting in the tall grass.

Felix was there, awaiting us.

"Where is Mr. Turner?" I asked.

"Already gone in," he said. "Mr. Clayton, you should go join them. Mr. McDonough is there, as well."

"You think it wise?" I asked.

Felix nodded. "They cannot go anywhere. And Mr. McDonough won't allow anything to happen."

Mr. Clayton looked at me. "What of our conversation?" he asked.

"Would you care to tell my brother?" I asked.

Mr. Clayton looked back and forth between the pair of us. "I don't know what sort of game the two of you are playing, but I am thoroughly convinced you are not exactly who you have claimed to be."

"That is where you are wrong, Mr. Clayton," I said. "We are who we have said we are. However...there is always more to a person than their relationships and connections, isn't there?"

Clearly, Mr. Clayton did not know whether to be frightened or angry.

"Tell him what you told me of Mr. Ward," I said.

Mr. Clayton, though reluctant, did fill Felix in on all of the information he had given me.

"Mr. Turner told me much the same," Felix told me after Mr. Clayton made his way back into the drawing room. "Though he did not seem nearly as suspicious of me as Mr. Clayton did of you."

"I think Clayton has changed his mind entirely," I said. "I wondered if he had begun to regret siding with Mr. Ward earlier this evening, before everything occurred with Mr. Lee. I can't quite explain it, apart from a look I saw on his face. He was clearly worried. He did not share the same smug attitude the others did."

Felix nodded. "It will be good for Mr. Carter to have someone else on his side," he said. "In fact, I wouldn't be surprised if they all abandon Mr. Ward when the truth comes out." He glanced toward the door. "Are you certain you are ready to tackle this?"

I shrugged, but a shiver ran down my back as if I'd stepped out into an icy storm. Perhaps I was preparing to do just that, in a way. "I don't know, but it seems that everyone is pointing their fingers at Ward. I wondered about him from the beginning. How could I *not*? His obvious hatred toward Mr. Carter was clear. In a way, I don't think it really could have been anyone else."

I sighed, shaking my head. "Still...something doesn't quite feel right about all this," I said. "The big question we have yet to answer is why Mr. Lee was the one killed. Yes, I understand he had been involved in some dark business deals. Yes, I understand that he and Mr. Carter had a falling out. But why him? Doesn't all of the trouble seem to keep going back to Mr. Carter, not Mr. Lee? It's as if we are fighting two different problems, but they don't match up."

"Why kill Mr. Lee when the hatred was directed at Mr. Carter?" Felix asked. "There does indeed seem to be a great disconnect between the murderer and the victim."

I frowned. "It does not add up, does it?"

"No..." Felix said. "We are still missing something."

"The only clue we have, really, is that it happened when the lights went out," I said.

"Which no one could have anticipated," Felix said. "I asked Mr. Turner about that, and he said the electricity hardly ever goes out in the city like this. He couldn't remember the last time."

I nodded. "So that was not planned or accounted for."

"It was simply taken advantage of," Felix said.

"Right..." I said. "It would be much easier to commit murder in the dark, which is often times why it happens in alleyways and at night, right? However..."

I looked up at him, something shifting back into focus in my mind. I snapped my fingers.

"What if it is not just the victim who was impaired by the darkness, but the murderer?" I asked.

Felix frowned. "They seemed to do an all right job," he said. "They killed him without getting caught, didn't they?"

"Right, but what if they didn't see the *right* person?" I asked. "Were you not telling me earlier that you mistook Mr. Lee from the back for Mr. Carter? And then when Mrs. Carter stumbled on the body, quite literally, she burst into tears because she thought it was her husband.

Both men had a certain resemblance, which would have been made stronger in the darkness."

Felix's mouth fell open, and he nodded. "Of *course*," he said. "It should have been obvious!"

"Mrs. Carter was *right*!" I said. "Come on, we have to go tell Mr. Carter right away!"

By the time we reached the dining room a few minutes later, sharp pains shot through my chest with every breath I drew in. We slowed just as we reached the door, and didn't even wait for the servant to open the door for us. Thankfully, the Carters were still barricaded inside.

"Mr. Carter," I panted. "They – they thought it was you."

Mr. Carter rose from his seat, his brow furrowing. His wife, seated beside him at the table, lost most of her color. "What do you mean?" he asked. "Has something else happened?"

"No, sir," Felix said, straightening up and trying to compose himself. "No. What we mean to say is that the killer mistook Mr. Lee for you."

Mr. Carter's expression hardened further. "I don't understand..." he said. "They meant to – to kill me?"

"Darling, this is what I was trying to tell you!" Mrs. Carter exclaimed.

"It was never about killing Mr. Lee," I said. "In the dark, whoever did this thought they were attacking you. Mr. Lee was killed entirely by mistake."

Mrs. Carter gasped, but I could see some of the relief on her face. Her husband might have been the target, but he was not ultimately the victim.

"This *cannot* stand," Mr. Carter said, stomping around

the table with all the force of a man seeking righteous vengeance. "I will find who did this, and – "

"No need, sir," Felix said. "I think we have already found him."

He stopped dead, and Mrs. Carter jumped to her feet. "Who is it?"

"Mr. Ward," I said.

Mr. Carter's face darkened. "I am ending this. Now." He snatched his antique sword from the table, and strode out of the room

"My dear, no!" Mrs. Carter said.

"Don't worry, Mrs. Carter," I said, shouting over my shoulder as I hurried out the room after him. "We won't let him do anything foolish!"

That is, if we can stop him...

13

"I am coming with you!" Mrs. Carter cried, chasing after us.

Felix slowed to look back at her, and then up the hall at her husband, who had begun to brandish his sword, shouting down the hall, "Ward? There is unfinished business between us!"

"You catch him," I told Felix. "I will try and – "

Mrs. Carter tried to dart past me, but I jumped out in front of her.

"Mrs. Carter, please, this is not safe," I said.

She pushed against me, trying to get around. "No, you cannot stop me," she said, tears in her eyes once more. "My husband needs me – "

"Your husband is not thinking clearly right now," I said. "Felix is going to talk him down before he has a chance to confront Mr. Ward. Trust me, the best thing you can do for your husband is to remain out of this."

She stopped fighting, and glared at me, with a look like daggers honed to a sharp point. "And what if something *does* happen, and I could have been there to stop it?"

"What if something goes horribly wrong, and you both end up dead?" I snapped, holding her fast. "What of your children? Do you really want to risk them losing both their parents?"

"I cannot let him go into danger alone!" she cried. "Do you really expect me to sit by and allow it to happen?"

"No," I said.

"Have you ever loved someone, Miss Crawford? Known that without them, your whole life would – would be ruined?" she asked.

I caught sight of Felix slipping around the corner at the end of the hall after Mr. Carter, who was quickly outstripping him.

I didn't know what I would do if I lost my twin.

Then Eugene passed through my mind, and my face colored. Our relationship was unclear, unresolved, and still the thought of something happening to him when I could have interceded made my insides ache.

"...Yes, I have," I said. "And I understand."

"Then do not stop me," she said, giving me another shove, and hurrying down the hall after her husband.

I groaned, but started after her. Who was I to stop her? Surely, she had to know the risks. I had spelled it out for her, and it only seemed to make her more determined. I wouldn't have wanted anyone to stand in my way, either.

I rounded the corner, thankful that Lewis had sent another servant through the halls with more candles, making the way at least somewhat more navigable. Mr.

Carter, however, who knew the house, had reached the drawing room before the rest of us did.

When I finally caught up to him, Felix, and Mrs. Carter, the confrontation had already begun.

"I know it was one of you," Mr. Carter was saying, sweeping the point of the sword across the room, pointing to each man in turn. "There is no other possibility. There is no way out, is there? You're trapped here. And you are at my mercy."

His face was red, his eyes flashing. Having been pushed to his limit, he now looked like a dangerous lunatic, despite the understandable reasons for his anger. How were we going to stop him from doing anything he would regret? If the situation wasn't deescalated, it could be Mr. Carter himself who would be hauled off by the police, in the end.

My throat tightened, and I looked around at all the faces of the men in the room.

"What are you going to do?" Mr. Turner stammered. "Cut – cut us down where we stand? Then you would be no better than whoever it was that killed Mr. Lee!"

"And my conscience would be clear," Mr. Carter said. "Because not only would I be avenging Mr. Lee, but I would be putting an end to the danger for everyone."

"Two wrong actions do not make a right, Carter," Mr. Clayton said, warily.

"Don't any of you try to tell me about what is wrong," Mr. Carter said, his head snapping toward Mr. Clayton.

Mr. Clayton took a full step back, holding his hands up in the air. "Carter, I have changed my mind. You have been right about everything with the company, all along. I never wanted anything like this to happen – "

"You think I am going to believe you now?" Mr. Carter barked. "You are a coward, Clayton, if you think you can change your mind when the tables have turned."

I glanced at Felix, who watched the situation unfolding with obvious concern.

Should we intervene? Or let it play out?

"We will all learn the truth..." Mr. Carter said, looking around the room again. Then he started to laugh...a sound which grew and grew. Soon, his laughter filled the room.

A shiver ran down my spine. I glanced at Mrs. Carter, and her face had gone slack.

Had Mr. Carter lost his mind? Had the fear gotten the better of him?"

He appeared to notice for the first time that his wife was in the room, and at that, his laughter quickly quieted.

"Did I not promise you that I would handle this situation, from the beginning?" he asked her.

Mrs. Carter stared at him as if he were a stranger.

"While I appreciate that you cared enough for me that you sought help, it was unnecessary to hire these two detectives," he said, indicating Felix and I.

The temperature in the room changed as eyes shifted toward my brother and me.

Well, thank you for that, Mr. Carter. What if we were not entirely ready to reveal our secret?

Mr. Carter turned back around to the other men. "How surprised are you to learn that your presence in this way is precisely as I would have wanted? In truth, the situation could not have worked out any better in my favor."

Now I really do think he's lost his mind.

"You expect us to believe you have orchestrated all this?" Mr. Ward asked. "That you somehow knew this was going to happen?"

"Would it truly be so unlikely?" Mr. Carter asked. "I know you, all of you. I know your dealings, your tendencies. You think I am nothing but a fool, yet I can assure you that as much as you have been watching me, I have been watching you."

Mr. Ward shifted uncomfortably, back and forth on his feet. Mr. Turner pushed his glasses up his nose, dabbing at sweat along his hairline.

"Allow me to enlighten you, since I have the control now," Mr. Carter said, lowering the sword, but keeping a tight grip on the hilt. "A point has been brought to me that makes a great deal of sense. Mr. Lee died in vain, it seems. For whoever it was that killed him made a blunder...they mistook him for me and struck down the wrong man."

An uncomfortable silence spread through the room, like a churning fire, ready to burst with steam. Something dark hung in the air, something sinister ready to launch itself. But like a pair of eyes watching from the deepest darkness, it could not be seen, only sensed.

"You see...one, or perhaps a few of you, know that my family has been receiving threats over the past number of weeks," Mr. Carter said. "They have been a nuisance, and a constant source of agony for my wife. Do not think I didn't take them seriously, darling. In fact, I have not rested until I came to this conclusion...and found a proper solution."

Mrs. Carter shifted uncomfortably nearby, and when

I looked at her, I noticed her fingers dug into the flesh of her arms.

"Allow me to tell you, gentlemen, that I happen to have information about you, information that I know full well you would rather remain buried, secrets of your dastardly doings, just as I said at dinner. However, it isn't just about *one* of you. No, I have something on each of you. Something that would ruin you."

"You are taking to blackmail?" Mr. Ward scoffed. "How does this make you any better than the rest of us?"

"Do you really have any room to speak right now, Ward?" Mr. Carter demanded loudly, rounding on him. His voice reverberated through the room, only rivaled by the hammering torrent of rain on the roof several floors overhead.

I swallowed hard. The atmosphere in the room had grown heavy, like the still humidity of the air before a storm. Something was about to happen, and every muscle in the room seemed primed for it, aware that danger loomed close.

"Carter...do you really think this is the best way to handle things?" It was Mr. Clayton, who had seemed to find his courage, at least enough to break the heavy silence.

Mr. Carter's head swiveled toward him. "Is there any further that this could go?" he asked. "I cannot see how anyone could have missed this, but Mr. Lee was murdered in my home, not two hours ago. Every decency has been superseded, overlooked, entirely ignored, and you expect me to allow the person who killed him to simply...walk free? Without consequence?"

"You should allow the authorities to settle this," Mr.

Turner said, wrapping his arms around himself as if to hide himself from the rest of us.

Mr. Carter laughed. "It was always going to come to this. Come now. We all know it. The situation was reaching a boiling point. It has been for some time. Shall I show you why this was always going to be the inevitable end?"

He turned his back on the others, which made the insides of my stomach turn summersaults; *why in the world would you leave yourself so open to them?* He strode to a writing desk tucked into the corner of the room, which had been left mostly in the dark. He yanked the long, narrow drawer open, not caring to be gentle. The contents within jostled around, and he snatched a stack of wrinkled envelopes from within. He strode with purpose to the open space where he had been standing, and tossed them haphazardly onto the floor.

The letters and torn envelopes floated and swirled through the air, each with a mind of its own, the papers fluttering like the wings of a bird rustling. They landed on top of each other, a visual representation of the chaos that pressed in on us from all sides.

I took another glance at Mrs. Carter. The look in her eyes told me she was beginning to question the sanity of her husband.

Mr. McDonough, who had moved to stand near her, looked ready enough to spring into action. I noticed his eyes darting around the room, likely trying to assess the best points for tactical advantage. *Something I should be doing, as well.*

"Feast your eyes, gentlemen, upon some of the threats

that my family has been receiving over the past few months," he said.

"Months?" I heard Mrs. Carter murmur, and her eyes grew larger.

This must have been going on far longer than even she knew...

"Death threats, threats of property damage, threats to my children, threats to my wife..." he said, jabbing his heel into some of the papers, swirling them around one another like some strange soup. "You all thought I was going to take this? To simply ignore it? Well, it seems that you don't know me, do you? You have failed to *really* understand me."

I eyed Mr. Ward, whose face had turned scarlet. He looked as though he might explode, his eyes bulging, his fists trembling.

"Why don't we all just admit that whoever killed Mr. Lee was actually trying to kill me?" Mr. Carter asked. "The man died for no reason, apart from what I can only assume to be a blunder on your part. So, well done for that, chaps. You made a mistake...one that will likely cost you your lives."

Mr. Clayton looked as though he were ready to be sick, clinging to the back of an armchair with a death grip. Mr. Turner's face had turned to stone, and if I could not see the shallow rise and fall of his chest, I might think he was simply a statue recreation of himself.

"You might as well confess who did this," Mr. Carter said. "You aren't leaving. You *can't* leave. And I won't *allow* you to leave until I know who is responsible. Who killed Mr. Lee?"

If silence could be deafening, then this was the

moment we all lost our sense of hearing. I strained to hear any change in the room; any subtle cough, any clearing of the throat...

"No? Can't say I'm surprised, really..." Mr. Carter said. "I hope you realize that I was gracious to you, for a long time. But now, I plan to share what I know of each of your deeds with not only the police, but with the company's major shareholders. All I have left to ask now is...was it worth it?"

The question hung like a weight tied to the neck of a man about to be thrown overboard.

"You might as well come clean," Mr. Carter said. "One way or another, I will make sure the truth is known."

No one moved for some time, until Mr. Ward fixed his hand to his lapel, and took a step forward.

"Well, Mr. Carter, you certainly seem to think you have us figured out...but have you stopped to consider that we might very well be more determined than you would hope? That we might not roll over and beg for forgiveness as you seem to expect?"

Felix tensed beside me. The simmering pot had nearly reached its boiling point, and soon it would overflow.

Mr. Ward sneered, sliding his hands into his pockets, rocking back and forth on his heels. "You see, we have indeed wanted you dead. That has been our plan from the start. We made a mistake, certainly. That matters little in the grand scheme of things, however...because we can finish the job now."

I held my breath, as Mr. Ward looked around the room at Felix and me, Mr. McDonough, and Mrs. Carter. "A pity there are so many witnesses who will have to be eliminated, as well," he said. "But it will not be difficult to stage a break-in, after the fact, and create the appearance you were all murdered in some sort of robbery attempt."

"That will never work," I protested. "You can't take down all of us and, even if you could, the police would never believe your story."

Mr. Ward blinked at me with cold eyes that suddenly reminded me of a reptile. "You may be right about that, Miss Crawford. But let's just see, shall we?"

14

Someone shouted. Someone else screamed.

The leg of a chair snapped. A table toppled over with a *crash* against the floor.

Before I knew what had happened, Felix grabbed me and pulled be down behind a shallow sofa along the wall, hiding me from view.

"What are you – " I protested.

"Stay down!" he barked, and disappeared from sight again.

My heart slammed against my chest as I tried to gather my bearings, but there was no sense to be made of the shouts and grunts and banging happening.

I sat up on my knees and peered over the top of the sofa, and my heart nearly stopped as I could not see anyone. A grunt, quickly followed by a command of "Don't move!" drew my attention toward the floor. I could just make out the top of Mr. McDonough's head, and Mr. Carter wrestled Mr. Turner, who seemed to be losing the fight rather quickly.

Mr. Ward somehow matched Mr. McDonough's strength, and managed to wrangle himself free from his grip. He got up on his hands and knees, panting, and snatched a lamp from a nearby end table. He chucked it toward Mr. Carter, but missed as it sailed past him... toward my head.

I ducked behind the sofa again, the lamp slamming into the wall above me, shattering into dozens of pieces. I covered my head, and dust settled in my hair. I frantically brushed it free, the fiery surge of fear pulsing through me, making each sound sharp, each sight brilliant and detailed.

BANG!

My heart stilled, and fear stabbed me. *A gunshot? But how?*

I hesitated, terrified of what I might find. Where was Felix? Where had he gone?

Slowly, I crawled to the edge of the sofa and peered around it, some of the broken glass on the floor piercing the tender flesh of my palm. I ignored the sharp pain, which seemed dull in comparison to the dread I felt.

I nearly cried out with relief as I noticed the hem of Felix's jacket just peeking out from one of the shelves; he must have hidden himself when he saw the gun produced. As if my gaze had called out to him, he stuck his head around the shelf just long enough to make eye contact with me before disappearing again.

At least he is all right.

I shifted my gaze just in time to see Mr. Ward, who held a smoking pistol in his hand, a look of smug success on his face, being tackled by Mr. McDonough.

He's shot Mr. Carter!

I jumped to my feet to see the damage, only to look wildly around for a dead body. It was nowhere to be found.

"Clever, Ward. I should have checked you for weapons earlier," Mr. Carter said, standing from a place beside the fireplace where he must have taken cover. A long scratch gleamed across his forehead, a thin trickle of crimson trailing his eyebrow. He brandished the sword, walking over to where Mr. McDonough held Mr. Ward against the floor, his arms splayed out on either side.

Mr. Carter looked about the eastern side of the room, and nodded before looking back down at Mr. Ward. He rubbed his nose along the length of his forearm. "Hard to tell if you're any good as a shot, though, seeing how the bullet ended up in the wall."

I followed his gaze, and sure enough, a hole the size of a knuckle had punctured the otherwise pristine cherry blossom wallpaper just to the right of the writing desk.

Mr. Carter kicked the pistol from Mr. Ward's hand, sending it scattering across the room. At the same moment, Mr. Ward let out a terrible cry; Mr. Carter's kick must have injured his fingers. Mr. Carter appeared unmoved, looking down at Mr. Ward, and continuing to clutch his sword in his hand.

"Is everyone all right?" I asked, looking around.

"Mrs. Carter is safe," Felix said. "I pushed her out into the hall."

"I'm – I'm still here!" came her trembling voice.

"Good, stay out there," Mr. Carter called, brushing some of his hair from his face, streaked with blood and sweat. "You don't need to see any of this."

"Easy, now, Carter..." Mr. McDonough said through

clenched teeth as he held Mr. Ward against the floor. "You don't want to add yourself to the number of people the police will have to haul away. Anyway, they will need to hear his confession."

Mr. Carter debated for a moment. "Fine," he said. "Tie him to the chair for all I care."

The pistol had come to rest just a short distance away from me. I made to fetch it when a rustling on the carpet near the door caught my eye. I noticed Mr. Turner shuffling on his hands and knees toward the door, a long gash across his shoulder, his sleeve in tatters.

I slipped out from behind the sofa, and stepped in front of his path.

Slowly, he frowned up at me.

Lewis appeared at my shoulder, and without ceremony, scooped Mr. Turner up by the elbow and yanked him back into the room.

"No, please..." sputtered Mr. Turner miserably.

I snatched the pistol up, and turned it over in my hand.

Felix produced a pair of chairs in the center of the room, along with the ties that had belonged to the drapes along the back wall.

Mr. McDonough threw a disgruntled Mr. Ward, who was still cradling his hand, into one of the chairs, while Lewis shoved Mr. Turner down beside him. Felix made quick work of the men's hands, tying them both behind themselves.

"There, now..." Mr. Carter said, standing before them, eyeing both men. He straightened and looked around. "Wait, where's Clayton – "

"I am here..."

Mr. Clayton stood from behind the sofa, his voice weak.

"Don't – don't shoot," he said, eyeing the pistol that I held in my hand. I wasn't even pointing it at him, but the sight of it seemed effective enough. "Carter, I had nothing to do with any of this. If I had known that – that it would come to this, I never would have – "

"You can grovel later," Mr. Carter spat.

"I think he means it," I said. "I spoke with him."

Mr. Carter looked at me, and I could still see the decision about whether or not to trust me in his gaze. Then he snapped back at Mr. Clayton. "You wish to prove yourself innocent? Tell me what happened."

"No, Clayton, you mustn't – " Mr. Turner began.

"Quiet, Turner," Mr. Carter ordered.

"From what I understand..." Mr. Clayton said in a shaky voice. He paused and shot Mr. Ward a wary glance. "It – it was Mr. Turner who killed Mr. Lee."

Mr. Turner let out a wail of lament, his head hanging to his chest, his shoulders shaking.

"Mr. Turner?" Mr. Carter repeated.

"I – It wasn't my fault," Mr. Turner burst out. He rocked back and forth in his chair. "Ward made me do it!"

Mr. Ward growled like a cornered mongrel.

"Let me guess..." I said, striding forward, the pistol gripped in my hand. "You wanted Mr. Carter dead so that you could take his spot in the company? That way you could all draft whatever new terms you wanted?"

Mr. Ward sneered as he looked up at me through his dark eyelashes, his bald spot gleaming with sweat. "Do you think I should commend you? Anyone with any sense could figure that out. Yes, it was my idea to kill

Carter, and Turner and Lee were in on it from the beginning. When you invited us here, it seemed too good an opportunity to miss."

"You hadn't planned on the storm or the lights going out," Mr. Carter said.

"No, but we would have been fools not to take advantage of it," Mr. Ward said with a nasty chuckle. "What better place than the pitch darkness where no one could see a thing anyway?"

"Well, your plan went south, because I am still standing here," Mr. Carter said. "Even after you tried a second time."

"So you thought the dark would help you get away with it?" I asked. "The dark would make the murder look like an accidental fall or some such, and you wouldn't have to worry about having the police on your trail."

"And because you couldn't see well, you mistook Mr. Lee for Mr. Carter," Felix said, coming to stand beside me.

"You are an utter fool, Turner," Mr. Carter said, shaking his head. "Why would you listen to him like this?"

Mr. Turner shook his head. "I'm sorry – "

Suddenly, Mr. Ward stood from his chair, another gun in hand, this one much smaller than the other. It must have been hidden up the sleeve of his coat.

Evidently Felix didn't tie Ward's hands as securely as I thought!

"Who has the last laugh now, Carter, eh?" Mr. Ward barked, pointing the gun squarely at Mr. Carter's chest.

I didn't hesitate. I lifted the pistol in my own hand, pulled the trigger, and felt my whole arm shift backward at the shoulder, like an earthquake raced along the length of the limb.

A cry let me know that I hit my target, and I stared in horror as Mr. Ward stumbled backward, flopping down onto the chair he had just left, and grabbed for his shoulder. Instantly, blood began to bloom in the spaces between his fingers.

A chill swept through me. I hadn't thought. I had simply acted.

I watched Mr. McDonough and Mr. Carter wrestle the other gun from his hand. There would be no way they wouldn't look for other weapons, now.

"Are you all right?" Felix asked, gently taking the pistol from me. I relinquished it without hesitation.

"Yes…" I breathed, but a knot had twisted around my heart, making it hard for me to breath.

I had been trying to stop Mr. Ward from killing Mr. Carter. In that moment, my body and mind had moved automatically. On instinct.

But to my horror, I realized I hadn't simply been trying to stop Mr. Ward.

I was…going for the kill.

15

"I think I am ready for a proper rest..." I said, sipping lemonade on the terrace of Cousin Richard's estate. The first sun in weeks shone in the blue sky above, brilliant and warm.

It seemed that everyone was looking for an excuse to be outside, so the gardens were being pruned and tended to by every available hand, the fountains cleaned, and a deluge of servants kept asking after what we needed. I had my lemonade refilled more times than I could count, and young William had managed to convince nearly half a dozen servants to play kickball with him out in the open stretch of grass near the hedgerows.

"And here I was, thinking we were settling in to do just that," Felix said as yet another servant offered him a plate of light, cool cucumber sandwiches. He graciously accepted a few.

I smirked at my twin, and settled back into my chair with a sigh.

It infuriated me that the knots around my heart had

not yet lifted since returning from Mr. Carter's estate. Since the encounter with the pistol in the drawing room, I had not felt settled. Not even when the rains had begun to clear and the police were sent for. I felt no relief as they dragged Mr. Ward and Mr. Turner from the closets they had been locked in for everyone's safety. Even after Felix and I had managed to get home the following afternoon, I had continued to feel uncertain.

Almost a full week had passed since then...and I could not entirely relax.

"You're thinking about it again, aren't you?" Felix asked.

"What?" I asked, looking at him over the top of my lemonade glass.

"Shooting Mr. Ward," Felix said. "You did the right thing, Lil. There is no reason to dwell on it."

"Yes, but Felix, I meant to kill him," I said. "I wasn't aiming for his shoulder, not deliberately."

"You've said this already," Felix said, taking a bite from his fifth cucumber sandwich. He smacked his lips a bit. "But you *did* miss anything vital, and you *did not* kill him. So why are you still worried?"

"Because – " I said, my eyes narrowing. "My *intention* was to kill him."

"Your intention was not to kill him," Felix said. "Your aim was self-preservation, and to save everyone else from a terrible situation. It was the right thing to do."

I sighed, shaking my head. "The trouble is that I didn't care whether I killed him or not."

"And what if you had?" Felix asked, staring at me. "Would it have changed the fact that you were doing what you could to protect everyone present?"

I grimaced, looking away.

"If you hadn't, then what would have happened?" Felix asked. "He would have killed Mr. Carter for sure, and then likely attacked anyone else nearby before someone finally managed to take him down anyway. At least your actions spared him his life."

"I suppose," I said.

Just then, Richard started up the shallow steps of the terrace toward us, wiping a small towel over the back of his neck. "My word, you always forget just how warm it can get this time of year..."

"Richard, a moment," Felix said.

"Certainly," Richard agreed. A servant appeared with a tall, glistening glass of lemonade, which he accepted with thanks.

"How likely is it that a gunshot would kill you?" Felix asked. "How direct would the shot have to be?"

"Well, typically it isn't the bullet that kills, but the blood loss afterward," Richard said, his brow furrowing. "If the shot were not anywhere vital, there is a decent likelihood the victim would live. Why do you ask?"

"See?" Felix asked. "It is unlikely you would have killed Mr. Ward anyway."

I sighed. "That isn't exactly what he said. But I suppose this is just something I will need to deal with over time."

"You're still struggling with pulling the trigger, I see," Richard said.

I looked away.

"You feel as if you are suddenly a stranger to yourself," Richard said. "You are surprised that you could be capable of doing such a violent thing without thinking..."

I did look up at that. Was that really what troubled me? That I felt like I didn't know myself suddenly?

Richard continued, "It might seem like you are sharing your mind with someone who has a violent tendency that could rear its ugly head at any time, but I can assure you...that sort of determination is something everyone feels when put into such dire circumstances. You will only see *that* form of yourself again when the danger is so great that side of you has no choice but to reappear."

I looked out over the garden, and finally it seemed that peace was able to pierce the thorny knots around my heart.

"It amazes me how brave you were, Felix," I said, no longer wanting to examine my shortcomings. "You had the quick thinking to push Mrs. Carter out of the room and away from danger, yet you did not escape yourself."

Felix shrugged. "I could hardly have fled for my life, dashing off down the corridor and leaving the rest of you to fend for yourselves, could I?"

I smirked at the somehow comical image that presented, but my smile quickly faded.

"Sometimes we must put our fears behind us and push forward," Richard said. "As they say, bravery is not the absence of fear, but the willingness to do what must be done despite the fear."

Felix nodded, suddenly thoughtful. "I suppose I understand that better these days than I ever used to...Of course, it helps that facing down murderers isn't as frightening as handling colleagues in Father's business."

Richard laughed. "You have the right understanding of it," he said.

"Both we Crawford siblings have faced fears, of late," I said. "And it seems to have changed us."

Felix regarded me. "I suppose it has, in a way."

"Well, I would say that Mother and Father have accomplished their goal, then," I said, sitting back in my seat. "They sent you here so that you would change your mind about taking over Father's business. Now that you have honed your courage on murderers, you may soon be ready for that greater challenge."

Richard nodded. "I think you would be ready, Felix," he said. "You have a great deal left to learn, but I think you would make your father proud now."

I was certainly glad for Felix...but what of me? What had I learned? Had I really grown much at all?

"Not that I am in any hurry to go back..." Felix said, leaning back in his seat, tucking his arms behind his head. He turned his face up toward the sun, closing his eyes.

"Don't worry, I'll put you to work..." Richard said, clapping Felix right in the middle of his chest, which made him grunt and flinch.

As I watched Richard wander off, making his way back into the house, I felt a bit worn out. Maybe it was the sun... I closed my eyes.

"Thinking of Eugene Osbourn?" Felix asked. I didn't have to see his teasing grin to hear it in his voice. "Doesn't he arrive back tomorrow from his tour in the north?"

My cheeks colored and my eyelids snapped open. *Yes, he does.* "Perhaps," I admitted. "Am I expected to follow his every move?"

Felix laughed. "Well, yes, because I know that you do. There's no sense in hiding it, really."

I shrugged. "I wonder if we will hear from him."

Felix laughed again. "I assume you will be the first person he contacts. Won't he be surprised to hear of our recent exploits?"

My lips twitched upward briefly, but I didn't answer.

"Things look bright," Felix continued. "We have a great deal to look forward to. And I feel like I am finally ready to face it."

Does that mean no more nightmares for him? I hope so...

I sighed. I still didn't quite know what the future looked like for me, aside from spending my days pursuing ruthless killers. Where was I going? What was I going to do next?

I supposed I didn't need to answer those questions right now, but one thing was for certain.

It seemed there was one thing I was good at: solving crimes...and I knew I would continue doing it.

Continue the mysterious adventures of Lillian Crawford with "Murder Among the Silent Dead: A Lillian Crawford Murder Mystery, Book 6."

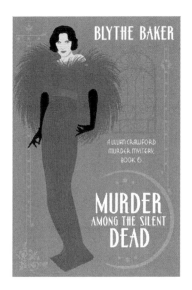

ABOUT THE AUTHOR

Blythe Baker is the lead writer behind several popular historical and paranormal mystery series. When Blythe isn't buried under clues, suspects, and motives, she's acting as chauffeur to her children and head groomer to her household of beloved pets. She enjoys walking her dogs, lounging in her backyard hammock, and fiddling with graphic design. She also likes binge-watching mystery shows on TV. To learn more about Blythe, visit her website and sign up for her newsletter at www.blythebaker.com

.

Made in the USA
Middletown, DE
25 September 2024